D1396681

Bent Dead in Beloit:
A Mystery

Tom McBride

This is wholly a work of fiction. Any resemblance of these characters to any actual persons living or dead is a total coincidence. The setting of the novel, however, is real. Beloit, Wisconsin is an interesting city on the banks of the Rock River, with a significant history, dedicated law enforcement, fine spirit of entrepreneurship, and excellent liberal arts college. As much as Chicago or London, it deserves a mystery novel.

"Heroism comes from two places: the wish to be special and the wish to save lives. The same result can occur from either motive." –Karl Malante, 2016

"Pardon me, you left your tears on the jukebox. And I think they got mixed up with mine." – George Strait, 1984

"Beloit is a lovely little college set in a lovely town near a lovely river." –George Hendricks, 1972

For John Nicholas:

The Last College Czar Standing

TABLE OF CONTENTS

The Beginning: Glock 1 and Glock 2

I have to begin a sad story somewhere and it might as well be with Roger's Glock, and mine. We both carry them. We're cops. They're the same make and model. You'd think they were the same. Well, they're not. I'm a college boy, you see—a failed college boy but still a college boy. And I took a course on language once, and the teacher said that the first rule is this: Cow 1 is not Cow 2. We use the same word for both cows, and that makes us think they're just alike. But cows can be different in big ways and small.

Same goes for our Glocks. I'll draw mine different. I'm more or less likely to fire mine. I'm more or less likely to fire mine at certain targets and people. I've got a Glock. Roger has a Glock. He's different from me. They aren't the same Glocks. Glock 1 is not the same as Glock 2. I learned that, though it was about cows, in college, and I also learned it working with Roger in Beloit, Wisconsin.

And my story is about a time when one of us fired and the other one didn't. This changed us for as long as we both shall live.

PART ONE: GOING BY THE BOOK

1: The Old River Town

I've been on the force here for eight years, and since I've done some college I managed to get myself promoted pretty fast. It's not that I'm any better than the other detectives. It's just that I talk prettier than they do, and this makes me sound like I know what I'm talking about.

Beloit is an old river town. It goes back to the 1840s and got set up for noble reasons. A bunch of pious souls from Yale came to "The West" to tame "The Wilderness," by which they meant drive off the Indians (our local flavor was the Blackhawks), start up a town, found a college, and establish a Congregational church. Now we still have all three minus the Blackhawks. They get plaques and place names, but there aren't any of them around here any more.

I grew up here and attended the local college, Beloit, where I had two years of philosophy and other courses. But for some reason I was never quite able to see myself as a college student. It just didn't seem applicable enough. It wasn't me. My father had been a railroad man, and my mother, until she found herself replaced by a robot or something, did bills at the phone company. They were working people. Reading Hume (he's this philosopher) all afternoon didn't seem like work. I felt worthless and out of who I think I am. My own folks told me to stick with it, even as they failed to give me any role modeling—don't recall my father reading Hume all afternoon—and so I quit. My dad spent his working hours, when he wasn't rounding up boxcars and fridge cars and tank cars, sitting in a caboose and reading why this was going to be the Brewers' year. I saw myself as more a man of the caboose than of the classroom, but I compromised and became a man of headquarters. It's never going to be the Brewers' year.

Oh, and did I tell you I fell hard for somebody. I wanted to marry her instead of philosophy. Silly me! I don't want to talk about it. It went down quick and bad. She was pretty shocked when I told her I was serious, and she said maybe, just maybe, we should curtail how often we lay eyes on each other ever again.

I joined the force. You could say if you wanted to that I did it out of civic duty. Beloit has this rep as a high crime town—mostly because we have a few too many bar fights. Guys'll get excited and break a beer bottle and wield it around like a shiv before we talk them down or just let them know, if we get there in time, that we'll aim for the beer bottle they've turned into a dagger but we might miss and shoot higher up. That usually does it. They don't call us peace officers for nothing. And so far none of them has been so drunk or high they've risked shooting a cop.

One key to being a good cop, I've always thought, is that you don't want to become a rogue cop—a wild west man—but you can play the part of a slightly rogue cop in order to appeal to people's self-interest if they aren't too smashed or high to know what it is.

I saw a little of that—the dwindling self-interest of drunks--before I donned my plain clothes. I wore the blue for a couple of years and knew that rational self-interest went down as the number of ingested brews went up. I was never that good at it, the uniform thing, I mean, though I did pull my piece a few times at the River City Tap or other places of solid citizenry. I had to arrest a woman once who'd taken a piece of another woman's nipple, nothing that wouldn't heal in ten or twelve years. So yeah, I've seen a few pictures from life's other side, especially when I was in the blue and black. I don't know what Hume would have made of all that. He might have said that I'm just imposing a story on all this and have no certainty that that's what really happened. He'd be right.

But even Hume wouldn't have wanted to be threatened by a bottle of Miller's Low Life with three sharp edges on what was left of its once pretty bottom. I think I've known that a long time and that's why I left college. I'm doomed to a life of blue-collar practicality, I fear. That's OK. I accept my fate. I'm even maybe a little proud of it. And Beloit's a good no B.S. town.

Anyhow, I didn't have to play traffic cop (but only for the 4th of July) and issuer of tickets for more than about three years until I moved up. Hume must have been good for something. Around the force they called me college boy sometimes. But I'm not a college boy. I never finished. I'm just Sergeant Jeremy Dropsky. I'm single. My partner is Roger Webb. He's married to a pretty woman. I'm pretty too if you mean by that pretty unmarried and pretty apt to stay that way. He has no college. But I always thought he was a better bad guy catcher than I am. They put us on cases where the bad guy isn't too obvious. Most of the time in Beloit it's pretty easy to spot the wicked ones.

But not always, folks: not always. Remember that, and you'll follow my tragic little story with much greater ease.

I'm burly with bad breath. Don't ask me to chase anybody for more than two blocks or you can expect me to apply for leave. With food I've blessed myself with a fat-fold face, around whose cushions you might (or might not) see a once-upon-a-long-time handsome guy, now doing a good imitation of a soft man in charge. The only thing thin about me is my hairline. I think what does my face in are those close-set eyes. Even if I was skinny those eyes would still look like they're headed for a bad collision. Say what you will, though, but I've got the logic of a good cop and the sarcasm of a scary one, at least some of the time.

Roger, now there's a good looking sucker: thin, not too tall; regular features; world-beater smile; diamond shape face, and the smile makes it look maybe a little bit like a fleshly version of the Hope Diamond. Priceless, the girls once said. But now he's got Mary with the short auburn hair, on whom I have an Olympian crush, who might find out some day that the Hope Diamond actually gets wrinkles in it that she can't iron out. She suspects it already, but that's for later, much later, she thinks. Well, she hopes so anyhow. They've been having trouble lately. Roger tells me about it all the time. He didn't grow up here. He came from Milwaukee, and he's got more street smarts than I do. He roamed the mean streets as a kid. Beloit's a comparative kindergarten. But every now and then we get something of interest.

That's what this story is about: something of interest.

We're close, Roger and I. We're buddies. I like his willingness to tell me secrets about his inner life, and he likes my willingness to scoff at a world that he is three quarters of the way to thinking is crap. He says I'm lucky to be a single dish of pudge, and I tell him that I'm lonely. I haven't broken the news that I love Mary. I won't. He tells me secrets. I don't tell him any. Maybe I don't think I have anything much to tell. Maybe I'm just secretive.

Roger and I did the police academy in Madison, shot at the dummies, learned the interview and crisis-tranquilizing techniques, and did a little study of the law. But there's part of this stuff you can't teach. That's the part Roger learned. That's the part I had trouble with. I'm a little like, maybe, a smart horse at a dinner party. I can use the right fork, but I have to practice harder, you know, seeing as how I have to lift it with a hoof. I can do good detective work. It just takes me longer to catch on to things. Roger, now he's real smart. He's quick. They say you have to have patience to be a good cop. Roger doesn't need patience.

That's one of the morals of this tale: Roger didn't need patience, and he didn't like it much either.

But though it takes me longer to get there, I think what I find is often finer stuff than what Roger finds. Or maybe I'm just jealous. I know I'm jealous of him being married to little Mary.

Now, though, they've got us heading out to talk to this woman who lives near Turtle Creek—what we sometimes call "The Golden Ghetto" around this working class town. Normally a uniform would handle this, but the woman says this is the third time she's had a peeping tom around, and once these things begin a pattern they call on Roger and me. It's not that there's anything we can accomplish of a constructive nature. These creepers peepers are often someone's imagination, and even if they aren't, they don't leave behind any leads. Nothing we can contribute out there.

There's nothing I can do about my wardrobe either: blue blazer, tan and winkled khakis sized large, a way too tailored shirt from Farm n' Fleet: snap on beige tie. But off we go anyhow.

***

"This woman says this is the third time," said Roger. "Either she's hearing things or it's the same guy or there are two or three different guys and they all want to see how the well-to-do in Beloit, Wisconsin live. I guess they think the back window's as close as they're ever gonna get."

"It's as close as we're ever going to get, too. Oh, wait: if we're lucky she'll let us come inside. We can sit down in the living room and tell her, in our own misleading way, that we haven't got a clue for sale or rent."

2: Tap Dancing Sitting Down

Well, Regular Roger and Gargantuan Jeremy (that's me) might want to get to the Golden Ghetto to tell the rich woman that we couldn't do anything about her so-called prowler. We might want to face the appalling fact of having to tell her that, no, we didn't have enough uniform help in Beloit to stake out her place, but we could ask the boys and girls to drive by a little more often. We might want to do, as I say, all this, but first we have to get past Rose.

You don't leave the station without passing by Rose. She weighs about two hundred fifty pounds. Her darkish blonde hair snakes raffishly down her back—it's about the only thin thing about her—and she wears big flowery dresses that manage to find their way down to just about her ankles. And she talks a streak and tap dances her feet the whole time she's carrying on. She's really good at it, too. The words and the feet are in sync. I can tell you that.

And unless it's an emergency, and we don't have too many of those in River City, we have to stop and chat for a bit. It's almost a regulation at headquarters. You got to respect Rose. She keeps the records. She knows every log in and log out. She's got enough dirt on your job performance that you'd better hear what she's got to say. Of course what she's got to say is never about your job performance.

What Rose has got to say is about Rose.

"Officers, I want to report a crime."

"What now, Rose," said Roger.

"What now, Officer Webb, is that I'm being swindled by my half-sister."

Rose had a nasal way of talking, as though she were insinuating information that was so sinister that it could not come directly from her mouth.

"So you and Susan aren't getting along again, right," I said.

"Bingo, Detective Dropsky."

"What's she done now?"

"She got into her wheelchair, motored all the way to South Beloit, stopped in at the Wendy's out there to plug in, had a big order of fries, and called a taxi to take her home."

"Doesn't sound like law-breaking to me, Rose, and I'm an x-spurt. Want me to spell that?"

"Well, Roger, that just shows how little you know about the law. If somebody is squandering the family fortune on needless trips and fries and expensive cab rides, there should be some law that's being broken."

"There isn't, Rose," I said. "You need a civil lawyer, not a cop."

This went on for a while, and I guess it's time to tell you that it's mostly all joshing. Rose hates her half-sister—they've been thrown together by circumstance—and she has no sympathy for Susan as a paraplegic. The two of them, Susan and Rose, were on opposite sides of a struggle for Daddy's favors. I think Susan won, so when Daddy Robertson died, the will stipulated that Rose had to take Susan in if she wanted her share of the funds.

Imagine having two daughters: one severely handicapped and the other severely obese. No wonder Mr. Robertson died. But Rose at least was a cracker jack records keeper—not that she was in any position to be chasing crooks, but then neither was I much with my own full figure.

Anyhow, we had to stop to listen to her latest spat with her half-sister. It was summer, you see, so Susan probably got tired of hanging around their little apartment on north Prairie Ave and decided to head via her carriage for beautiful South Beloit, on the Illinois side. I guess for someone as housebound as Susan a voyage to the Land of Lincoln would be like, oh, going to Starved Rock State Park (downstate Illinois) for the rest of us. I hear it's pretty down there. Hear there's a Wendy's overlooking the Illinois River.

"So what do you think, guys? The next time this happens, could I get one of you guys to go pick her up?"

"No way," said Roger. "We've got bad guys to catch. We don't run no taxi service."

"Well, you know I could make it worth your while. Put in some fake overtime for you?"

"You don't really think we can be bribed do you, Rose—a couple of honest peace officers like us?"

"You might be honest, Jeremy, but you don't keep any peace that I know of. In Beloit we're too bored most of the time to even think about doing anything wrong. That's what keeps the peace."

"I don't like your logic. Boredom leads to crime."

"It does everywhere else. But not in Beloit."

I don't know if she had me there, or if Roger and I just needed to get on. But we laughed and seemed to agree.

Little did either of us know, then, that Rose's idea would be sorely tested, and fairly soon.

3: Trouble on the Turtle

Gloria Drabble showed us right away that she had a lot of life about her. She was over forty-five for sure, but affected being about thirty, and her act was damnably good. She'd dyed away any fledgling gray in her shoulder-length auburn hair, and she had a bouncy way of moving around. She'd called us because there was some little problem on the banks of Turtle Creek, near which her suburban Beloit home resided in seeming heart's content. Flow gently, sweet Turtle. But she was cheerful about the difficulty and almost apologetic for taking up our time. She was pert, you'd say, and had a good figure. For somebody who'd been afflicted with a so-called peeper she seemed pretty sure of herself—in command, almost, the way someone is in control of a cheerleading squad.

"So how many times do you think this person has bothered you?"

This was Roger. He seemed more interested than I was.

"Three. But you see, I can't be sure what it was. I heard rustling out of doors, and once I thought I saw a shadow at the window, and I'm pretty sure that when I asked who was there the shadow moved off fast. But maybe I'm seeing things. Maybe I'm just getting jittery in my old age."

This seemed designed to elicit from either or both of us a comment to the effect that she was hardly old. Truth was, she was more youthful than I was, though I was maybe seventeen years younger. I was born a heavyset old man. She had lithe written all over her from glossy forehead to pinky toe.

"Is there, uh, a man about the house? I don't mean to ask personal questions, but we need background, you see." This was Roger again. So far I hadn't offered even a syllable.

"No problem, officer. There isn't a man around. I'm separated from my husband. You may know him. He's Andrew Drabble, and he lives in Rockford. Well, is now at any rate. We've been living apart. He's got a sizable developer business, mostly land; buildings from the ground up."

"Well, this is just a routine question in an investigation like this." There: I'd finally said something. There's nothing quite like pretending in police work that you're interested in what you can't do much about. It gives the public comfort.

"OK," said Roger. "So maybe you can just show us, uh, the window where you saw this, this fellow. We can go outside and look around a little."

"Why don't I just take you over to the side of the house? The window was in one of the bedrooms."

"The house" was a sizable affair: Light brownish brick; split-level; four bedrooms, including a couple of bathrooms (odd) right off the beddy-bye. Mrs. Drabble led us outside to a slightly weedy section at the side of the house. Some of the bedrooms were up half a story, as befits a split-level, but this one, which she was in during the alleged incidents, was on the ground floor. I don't know why it was ill-mown. At the front of the house was a rock garden. Sometimes these people with rock gardens forget they have grass nearly everywhere else.

The heat was starting to mug me, and I started to wonder if Rose's sister Susan had had a big Coke with those fries of hers in South Beloit. I could have used a big Coke. But I have too many of those as it is.

Well, we looked around, right, and of course—you got it—we found no cigarette butts or jack boot prints. We found nothing at all. If there was a prowler about, he'd left nothing of himself behind. That's when I started to wonder if Roger was going to whip out his magnifying glass and start looking for clues, Sherlock Holmes style. He really seemed into this assignment. I thought it was a nothing sandwich.

Silly, stupid me.

We went back inside, to the cavernous living room, where Mrs. Drabble offered to make us coffee. We declined, though maybe I did so with a little more pep than Roger did. That was unusual. Most of the time Roger did everything with a little more pep than I had.

"I suppose it would be a lot better if Andrew and I were still living together. Maybe these sorts of people wouldn't come around if there's a man around the house. But he isn't here, and I don't know if he ever will be back here again. We just weren't getting it together. You don't want to hear about my personal problems."

Roger seemed to take the bait. He hadn't told her she wasn't an old lady, not with those looks, but she no sooner said that we didn't want to hear about her personal problems than Roger asked if he could hear a little bit about her personal problems.

"Again, Mrs. Drabble. We have to ask this. Is there any possibility, do you think, that your husband might have been this guy who might have been bothering you?"

Well, that did it. That's the sort of question we absolutely do NOT have to ask, especially on a first visit about what so far seemed to be nothing whatever.

"Oh, surely not. Andrew is very possessive. Well, he *was*. He lives high. He takes chances. He borrows too much. He brought off a big mall just south of Rockford with money he couldn't possibly pay back. But he did it. He likes to live high. He's a swaggering sort, you see. I'm sort of surprised you've not heard of him."

"Well, we might have seen his name in the Beloit papers every now and then." I said that. I thought that least I could keep the inane conversation going. The truth was, we didn't even know if there was a peeper. If there was, there wasn't anything much we could do about it. Now we're talking about an estranged husband's land deals. Roger is acting like a TV cop. At least Mrs. Drabble had her air conditioning going. Now if she'd just get me a big Wendy's Coke I'd be happy to listen to cop show dialogue for the rest of the afternoon, especially if she threw in a Hostess cup cake. Just one: I'm not gluttonous. I wondered what my old philosophy profs at Beloit College would think of me now.

Why would I care?

"Anyhow, prowling isn't Andrew's style. He doesn't do anything on the sly, except maybe borrow too heavily from the banks. I sometimes think he'd have been happier with a more line-crossing woman. I guess you'd say I'm a homey, law-abiding type. I finished Beloit College, you know. Got my degree in psychology. Came from Nebraska originally. Met Andrew while I was a senior waiting tables here, at the old Manor before it closed. He's ten years older. We hit if off. I really can't imagine why now. But we didn't marry for over a decade after we met."

Mrs. Drabble was keen on telling us her life story. My ears did perk up with the mention of Beloit College. Of course she wasn't there when I was. But we had trod the same turf once. She knew where all the Indian Mounds on campus were. So did I. We had that bond. But it was Roger, no college man at all, who was inducing all this—what should I call it—all this *content*.

"I grew up in a small town near the Platte River. We were always told that the Platte was dangerous. We shouldn't try to cross it or even swim in it unless our folks were around. So I learned to respect limits. That's never been Andrew's way. Maybe he wanted to marry me because he was looking for a good little girl to cleanse his life. What do you think?"

"I wouldn't know, ma'am," said Roger. Then he caught me in the side of right eye and added, "*We* wouldn't know." Thanks, Roger. Now how about we leave and get to Wendy's?

"Yes, well, officer, that makes two of us."

"Three of us." I blurted this out. I was starting to feel malicious. Being marginalized will do that to a man, especially a Coke-starved man.

Neither of them responded. I wasn't there.

But at this point I think even Roger was getting chagrined—a bit—and so he wound it up. He told Mrs. Drabble that the force couldn't post a uniform at the house all the time, but patrol cars would be riding by every hour or so during the nighttime for a while.

"Oh, thank you. I knew there wasn't much you could do. I didn't really supply many, what do you call them, clues."

"Leads," I said.

"Leads, yes." She acknowledged me!

"Well, we'd best be going. Call us right away if anything else comes up. Here's my card, and Jeremy must have his." I did. "And try not to worry. Nine times out of ten this sort of thing is absolutely nothing."

How did Roger know this? What research had he done on "this sort of thing?" I shouldn't have asked. Sometimes I wish I'd never gone to Beloit College. It's made me sensitive to illogic and empty talk. And I never even got a degree. And no one told me not to cross the Platte River, or even the Rock River, by myself at night. No one had to. I had better sense.

4: Dez on the Prowl

After our world-class police work with Mrs. Drabble it was near enough the end of the working day that I left a bit early for my little bungalow on St. Lawrence Avenue on Beloit's far west side. If you kept driving west for about three minutes you'd hit countryside and from there to various and sundry farms or even fancy farmettes. That's the only plush thing about my locale. My place isn't much. I was about as good with interior decorating as I have been with diets or women. But the Salvation Army couches and St. Vincent's lamps didn't matter all that much—yeah, the leather was worn and torn and the curtains were dirt yellow—because I have something even better than furniture from IKEA: *Dez*.

Did I tell you that Mrs. Drabble had a cat? She was a fat Persian who briefly looked in on the living room conversation about Mrs. Drabble's prowler. She (or he) withdrew almost as quickly as she'd appeared, whether in fright or boredom or decorum I couldn't tell—can you ever tell with cats—but then later pushed open a swinging door from the kitchen into the living room and paraded by us in some disdain. She wasn't alone. I too looked down with dismay on how Roger was handling this interview. I thought he asked way too many questions.

Anyhow, Dez is *my* cat. She's a Humane Society orange tabby, pretty small but quite fierce. Robins respect her. She goes out a lot. I fixed up a cat door. She was waiting for me when I got home. She wanted some food, but I swear she also wanted me to tell her what had happened at work. This is my whole theory of cats, you see. You can't tell what's going on with them, so you're free to imagine what's going on with them. In a way I could allow myself to be, with Dez, Roger himself. Roger was a good cop—organized and smart and perceptive—EXCEPT when he let his imagination do wind sprints. That had happened, I was sure, with Mrs. Drabble. It was as though he was to her as I am to Dez. Roger and I know nothing about what's really happening sometimes, and we'll never know so we're at liberty to fancy.

I've got a strange thing with Dez. I can impute to her all sorts of thoughts, while she can play detective in the neighborhood, where she's the chief prowler—that's right: she's the genuine peeper, unlike Mrs. Drabble's likely non-existent one. I can be the dreamy poet on my Goodwill Industries couch. She can be the cop on the beat. That's my escape. At work I'm the cop. Only at home can I make up stories and pretend I'm writing them in short lines of verse. This is verse you'll never want to see, which is why in this story I'm sticking to prose.

And all the stories are about what Dez sees. Sometimes, I swear, I have these slightly out-of-body experiences and aren't sure whether I'm telling Dez what she saw or she's telling me. I shouldn't be telling you all this. But I decided, after what's finally happened with Roger, to spill, and that's what you're reading now—my spillage.

First things first, however: I gave her Fancy Feast and while she was on her dainty feeding frenzy I told her all about how Roger had overdone it with Mrs. Drabble. Once a neighbor had threatened to call the police on me because Dez had climbed to the top of a tall tree in her yard and was upsetting her dogs. I told her I was the police, whereupon she added that I should be ashamed of myself and ashamed of my cat. I advised Dez never to do that again. I don't know if she listened, but I've not heard from the neighbor again. I'll bet my neighbor doesn't tell her dogs stories. Dogs just aren't blank slate enough.

So what does Dez see on her prowls? How far does she go? What does she do between nibbles of birds and field mice?

I'm sure she sees Roger and his wife Mary. They live a bit out of Dez's territory, true, but not that far, maybe only twelve blocks east near the old high school, the one that burned down in the 1950s. Dez gets in the tree near their kitchenette, and Dez listens to them talk and argue. And she knows that Mary is starting to wish she hadn't married Roger (the feeling is reciprocated), who's of course destined to be a really striking guy for another fifteen years but also fated to be a wounded drinker for at least that long. Roger's got anger issues. He drinks because he's angry, and he's angry because he drinks. And he's prone to magical cogitation. I could swear that he saw the Drabble business as a way out of a drab life. Better a Drabble existenc than a drab one? Forgive me. He thought the case was more interesting than it really was. He saw himself as a TV cop, looking in on some rich babe in 90210 instead of an early middle aged good housekeeper in 53511.

That's what I thought.

And now Dez is listening in the tree while Mary says:

"I didn't say you should stop spending 5 to 7 at the bars. I said you might think of spending 5 to 7s sometime with me instead. Not every day; maybe twice a week? Is that too much for you Roger?"

"I got a tough job. I need the time away. I need to tell Joe my life story. I need him to hit me with whiskey. I need to unlax. Is that too much for *you* to handle, Mary?"

"I guess not, Roger. Are there any women at this bar?"

"Of course there are. Do I talk with them every now and then? Yes. Do I sleep with them? No. And I'm here by 7 for dinner, and we have the entire night together. Don't we?"

"We do, Roger. We do. We watch the same TV shows. We commune over cable. Isn't that great?"

"I don't know what you want from me, Mary. You must think I'm some sort of cosmic hole you can jump into so that you can commune with the spirit of—I don't know—the spirit of what? You tell me, Mary. I'm right here, right now, and we're talking and I'm not at the bar tying one on with Beloit's most beautiful ladies and we're cable free and I'm all ears so you tell me, Mary: what do you want to commune with? How can I help? I am supposed to be the great cop. How can I help?"

"Forget it, Roger. You're a little drunk and a little mad. But I repeat myself. Just tell me what case you worked on today. Let's start our great intimacy with that."

"You really want to know? Mrs. Andrew Drabble of east Beloit, Turtle Creek area, thinks she's had three incidents of a prowler. She and Mr. Andrew Drabble are separated so she's by herself there. These incidents may or may not have occurred. Mr. Drabble may or may not be involved. We have absolutely nothing to go on. Oh, and Jeremy has given up on his latest diet. I knew you'd want to know that. So this is my life, Mary, and it's pretty much like dirty dishwater and I need escape and I need the booze and the bar and the cable. I don't need cosmic connections, Mary."

Dez is watching and Dez is listening, and Dez is a smart cat and is as silent as the tomb and undetectable, and Dez sees that Mary is a lovely, fetching mystic. She's short and slim and an intense brunette with hair shorn slightly above her shoulders. Chic to the third degree she is, in my humble opinion. Dez sees that she has a boyish, taciturn way about her and that she's not the sort of "bouncy all-woman" that Roger probably likes to get him a beer. Mary has unerring curiosity. She notices things. She's sensitive. Roger has brought out her nagging side—too bad. She's a little unconventional and knows antiques and works as a part-time auctioneer every now and then. She knows Roger has issues. She's also motherly. She will get him through this. But tonight, Dez notices, she's lost some patience. She's starting to think the patient is beyond help. But she's going to stick in. She sells watches in Janesville. It's a job beneath her intelligence. But surely Roger can be reached somehow. Mary isn't going anywhere. Neither is Roger, except to Mac's Tap and the TV room. He always makes sure to pay Charter Cable.

This Dez sees and hears, and tells me about. I am having microwaved tater tots with her report. Dez assures me that she has never been outside Gloria Drabble's bedroom window. Dez has no dope on that. So that lead's gone, too.

5: On Tap With Mac

Rose said, "Before you two officers go out for the day, I want to file a complaint."

It had been a couple of days since our rendezvous with Gloria Drabble, and Roger was still stewing about what to heavy-set indolent me was a non-event. He wanted to vent and had invited me to spend part of his precious two daily hours at Mac's Tap on 4th Street with him.

But now we had Rose. You couldn't get by her. There had once been an office pool on how long it would take her to rise from her office chair, which was on wheels. She was heavy, even heavier than I, and the wheels didn't help when it was time for her to get up and go home. But she could wheel herself into the ladies' room at any time. Even so, she was a lot more mobile than her half-sister was, or had been for years.

"Is this a complaint about us?" asked Roger.

"It's not. It's a complaint about my half-sister Susan. Maybe I should call her my half-ass sister Susan?"

"What now?" I asked.

"Is mental cruelty a crime?"

"No, it's a category in a civil divorce suit."

"It should be a crime. If I put in for time and a half for you boys will you make mental cruelty a crime?"

"If you do that," said Roger, "we'd do our best. That's all we can promise."

"Well, last night she got galloping on the accident that put her in her chariot. Our father was driving. Roads were icy. He'd had a few. I was home probably playing with my dolls. My mother— Susan's mother was my dad's first wife—was likely in the kitchen making vanilla pudding. She was always making vanilla pudding. We had lots of extract on hand. I'm telling you guys this because my mom's still alive, and you might want to bet your pensions on vanilla extract stock.

"Thanks for the tip—better than time and a half."

"Don't get cute, Buster." You wouldn't want Rose to fall on you on an icy sidewalk. No worries now: it was the dead of summer. "Anyhow, I had nothing to do with this accident. Daddy was lucky. He broke his arm. Susan hadn't a seat belt on. Daddy didn't make her. He'd had a few, like I said. The road was slippery. He was probably driving too fast. Susan's spine was crushed. End of story."

"Yeah, well, Rose, you've told us this before. What does this have to do with mental cruelty? Are you planning to divorce your father? Isn't he in assisted living now or something?"

"He is not, he's dead, but Susan's with me, as you know. So last night she went off on how it was all my fault. It wasn't our father's drinking. It wasn't that the road was glazed gut. It was that Daddy was so worried about me that he couldn't pay attention to his driving."

"What did she say he was worried about—where you were concerned, I mean."

"That I was still playing with dolls at age thirteen. Well, I did play with dolls for a long time. But you can't get from there to a crushed spine."

"Yeah, it does seem quite a long trip to make. Even we'll admit that, Rose."

"Right. But she's starting to make this trip every night. She rags on me about how it's all my fault. I hate her. I wish her chair was some sort of breathing apparatus."

"Would you pull the plug?"

Hell, yes, I would."

"OK, Rose. We'll look into this mental cruelty thing first thing tomorrow. Roger's got to have his Gator Aid Gin Milkshake for now, though. You've given us a lot to work with: mental cruelty, vanilla extract stocks, time and a half. You've given us more to work with than that Gloria Drabble woman did.."

Roger shot me a look. Rose cackled a mirthless laugh. We left for Mac's.

It was dirty and dark. I think some guys like to attribute a kind of manly evil to their local bar. If the same drinks were imbibed in the runway of a mall, they wouldn't be interested. I got a light beer—not an homage to a badly needed diet but just because I wasn't into booze that much—while Roger got his double gin fizz.

Joe McVey the barman himself brought our drinks over. His face looked like five inches of unpaved road; his hair parted in the middle so that the top of his head looked like a dry gulch bordered on both sides by a greasy polluted pond. He said, "Where ya been,

Roger? Haven't seen you in six weeks. What ya been doing these past six weeks?"

"Six weeks," Roger deadpanned. Joe's giggles did a pretty fair imitation of Mount Saint Helen's on a good day. "I like that one. Six weeks! Great joke coming from a cop!" He left us.

"I thought you were here every night now."

"I am, most nights, but sometimes I like to visit other bars in our fair city, Jeremy. Besides, Joe saw me just a few nights ago. Don't pay attention to that six-weeks crap. If I could, I'd arrest Joe for liver and brain disease. He doesn't know. I was just here, and he poured the drinks. Collected my money, too."

"OK, I see. That wasn't a bad joke. When I've heard it, though, it's been 'six months.' That's even better. I'm just saying."

Roger had different business to discuss, something far more grave than the art and science of low comedy. "Wish you wouldn't bust my balls about that Drabble business, partner."

I always found Roger a bit menacing. He was better built than I was; closer to the great unwashed than I was; had had no college and none of those sissified pretensions that I'd had for a while. He'd had much more sex. Mine was confined to a semi-pro in Fond du Lac. He was closer to the polluted ground waters. But he liked my sarcasm, I think; it was the only tough thing about me. I think he also knew I was smart, even if my smarts didn't always extend to being a cop. I knew regulations and procedures better than he did. He had more instinct.

"Sorry about that. I was mainly just joshing with Rose. I never quite know what to say to her. Is she kidding? I don't think so. She's gotten more ferocious over the past few months about Susan. I think it used to be complaining. Now I think she's into a Federal case. But she doesn't have the Feds behind her."

"Yeah, you're right about that. Anyhow, you and I have worked together for several years now. We've only been in one tight spot together, but you get a little close investigating burglaries and stolen vehicles and asking around the Merrill neighborhood about bad guys the Chicago cops are looking for, and bonding with all the grannies of the troubled kids and trying to do community policing and so on. I just want to be straight with you. I think there's something maybe big going on with this Drabble woman."

"But what? We're not even sure there's anything beyond her imagination. Might have been a prairie dog scratching its balls on the side of the house."

"Nah. My gut tells me it's something more than that."

"What does your gut tell you that is, Roger? My gut's a lot bigger than yours, but my gut can't find a thing."

"Oh, I'm pretty sure it's the hubby."

"Andrew Drabble, the Realtor of Rockford? Why? From what I've picked up here and there, this guy's so rich he could hire his own professional counselor to make an advance trip to the house and beg for her forgiveness for, for what? What did she say the marital trouble was?"

"She didn't exactly say. But she sort of hinted that she was too wholesome for him. I think he wants her to be a bad girl."

"What? He wants a woman into threesomes? Doggy style? What? You don't really know any facts for sure, Roger, and even if you did about their sex life, that doesn't get you a real prowler. Maybe it's a prairie dog wants her to go doggy style. Come to think of it, that would make more sense."

I'm not proud of this doggy talk, but I told you: I like cats better.

"Look, Jeremy, old pal. I sense this woman's in danger, OK? I've heard bad things about this Andrew dude. I don't like his looks either. I've checked back issues of the papers."

"OK, Roger. You're the man with the gut instinct. I'm the man with facts." I didn't tell him that my cat reported "facts" to me every night. He might get the wrong idea somehow.

"Yeah, well thanks, Jeremy. I think we should have a word with this Andrew Drabble."

"He'd only report us for harassment."

"Is that a fact?"

"No, that's only a strong possibility." In defense of my believing Dez's nightly cat reports, I'll insist right here and now, without Roger knowing it, that what Dez informs me about are all just strong possibilities and no more. I'm not crazy.

"OK, well, let's leave aside the particulars of the case for a moment, Jeremy. Don't you ever want to save somebody?"

I wanted to say, "Yes, Roger: your wife Mary." I did not.

"Uh, no, not really. But what does that have to do with the Drabble lady? I won't call it the Drabble 'case' because there is no case."

"I'm trying to make my life make sense, old pal. My life is mainly my marriage. My marriage doesn't make sense. Mary's been trying to belittle me."

I knew it. I knew Dez was accurate in her reporting. Here I've got to let you all in on a little secret. Most of what Dez sees I imagine, but what I imagine is based on personal observation. And Dez gets into this mix just beautifully. I've seen Roger and Mary out at this restaurant and that one. I've sometimes been with them. They've had me, the plump asexual bachelor, over for dinner. I've seen them interact. I've sensed things. I don't ever, ever, ever want to break this to Roger, but I may have a sounder imagination than he does. I don't see anything solid to imagine in the Drabble business. But he does.

Why?

"How's Mary trying to belittle you?"

"She doesn't respect me. She doesn't respect what I do. She doesn't respect how hard my job is. She doesn't respect how important it is to the peace around here. You and I both know that there's no peace in Beloit without us cops. Mary doesn't get that. She doesn't care. She just wants to link up with me. I'm not linkable. I don't fit Mary's plug.. She doesn't care. She keeps harping on it. I'm a man, not a goddamned emotional cable hook-up."

"Quite a speech, Roger. I doubt she's trying to dis you. She just wants the cop part to help make the living. Then she wants the man part after hours. She wants the 'gentle guy' part after hours. She wants you, like, to be complex, Roger. That's all."

I was truly grateful for all those Dez reports. They gave me a good grip on the Webb case, which I thought had a lot more to it than the Drabble case.

"I'm pissed at Mary, Jeremy. I'm really angry at her. I don't love her, not any more."

"I'd try to work it out, Roger."

"I know you sometimes think you're unlucky. You've never found anybody. But it could be worse. You could be in a shitty marriage. I am."

I thought that tonight, when I got home, and made myself a calorie-laden frozen dinner and topped it off with a giant economy size chips, and waited for Dez to return with her nightly account of pulsating Beloit life all around me, I'd take time to thank my lucky stars that I wasn't hitched to luscious boyish Mary Webb.

Yeah, right. The Rock River will sooner freeze over on the 4th of July.

6: Envying the Bounty

I'll readily admit to being besotted with Mary, and like all guys so smitten, I can point back to a single encounter branded on my memory. I once read about some Russian poet who said that he envied the waves because they had touched his beloved's feet while he had not and would not. Well, I sort of envied the paper towels in Homecare Pharmacy on Woodward Ave because Mary had touched the fat rolls of Bounty and had never touched, and would never touch, me. Roger was a man of extreme fortune, I thought, and to this day cannot fathom him finding himself distant from her.

I know a lot more now, though, than I did then.

Roger and Mary had had me over to dinner a few times—don't know whose idea it was to have the partner over for a meal—and I sort of enjoyed both those occasions because Mary's cooking is a lot better than Marie Callender's. But I didn't know Mary well. Looking back, I think my romantic yen for her precluded me knowing her too well. I don't know. Maybe Roger knew her *too* well. But I still believe that I could have known her very well and loved her until she or I or both of us were all over.

Not that she'd ever feel the same about me: I was basically shy and couldn't make up for it around her by being acid and sarcastic all the time. That wouldn't have worked for Ms. Mary. So with her, the few times I was with her, I had to stick to shy and leave my defense mechanisms at the door, right? So here I was: this timid and pudgy guy with a few face scars—after effects of an acne fed by banana splits—who happened to run into Mary one winter's day at Homecare.

I saw her first, but I'll say this, desperate man that I am: When she saw me she walked over to talk. She didn't have to do that. She could have just said hello and I'd have been over the moon and all the planets.

"Is this the place to shop or what?"

"Yeah, I like Homecare. It's got a little bit of everything, and they're all easy to find. Nicely spaced out...."

This was a banal thing to say, but I had to say something. Didn't I?

"And we can look at all their equipment for the elderly and injured and see ourselves in forty years, right?"

It was true. Homecare specializes in sales or rentals of wheelchairs and walkers.

Mary had given me an opening, and even a fat goof like me figured out to take it.

"I can't imagine you on a walker, Mary."

"Anything can happen to any of us, Jeremy. You're a cop. You should know that."

Mary had this sublimely clipped brunette hair. I worshipped that. I've thought about why. I think it has to do with confidence. She had the self-assurance to show her face and not try to distract anybody from it by some Niagara of follicles down her back. Unlike a lot of women she didn't have to worry about brushing her hair back—this has always annoyed me for some reason—and I also have a thing for Demi Moore in *G.I. Jane*. Mary resembled her. Or maybe I'm gay and don't know it—when you're overweight and without women maybe you even become gay (I don't know). Whatever: Mary delivered me to a little session of private madness. If you could translate the energy from her to me into fuel and lift I could flap my blubbery wings and fly to Des Moines, maybe even Denver.

Does this sound pubescent? No opinions, please.

I guess I just nodded when Mary said that as a cop I should know that even she could end up on a walker because she said something else.

"You and Roger must see things as cops that the rest of us don't know about. Roger never tells me any of it."

"He doesn't?"

Here I was, at that time anyhow, imagining that Roger spoke to Mary as I speak to Dez: that Roger and I both had our super-confidants. But with Roger, what? Not so much?

"He tells me very little about the job, Jeremy…only that he wants to be super-good at it."

"Wow! I didn't know. I mean, I wouldn't have thought so."

"What—that he wants to be good at the job?"

"No, not that, I knew that. I just meant I thought he'd tell you about our days…not that there's always lots to tell. There are domestic quarrels, probation violations, a lot of routine stuff. But I thought he'd give you the low-down."

Mary smiled. Her face went on like one of those photoelectric lights that glow when a foreign object comes into their path. I guess my "I thought he'd give you the low-down" was such an object.

But her smile, while glowing, was melancholy bright. It also had a touch of admonition in it, as though to say, "You really don't know Roger, do you, Jeremy. You don't know about marriage either, do you Jeremy. You're here at Homecare probably to buy some extra Twizzlers and hide from the world, right?"

"I guess you thought wrong, Jeremy. He doesn't."

Mary had the brightest, whitest teeth I've ever seen. If the mouth is a dining room her chairs were like from the Palace at Versailles or something. Really classy, I thought. I still do think.

I was in love with this woman. I am still in love with this woman. Oh, sure, I've got to give a point to Roger and realism. When you get to know someone, the bloom lifts, the dew melts, and all that trite stuff. Maybe I'm in love with this woman because I know I'll never really know her. Maybe I don't want to get to know her because I want to stay in love with this woman.

But I know one thing. I am in love with Mary Webb. I'd gladly have given Dez to Roger for a month to see more of Mary. We parted that day on cheery terms, each of us facing the snowy dark in our own probably incompetent ways. She had her Bounty. I had my Skittles. I'm sure she didn't envy the Skittles.

7: *Going By the Book with the Boso Bros*

Mary told me at Homecare that Roger never discussed his work with her. Well, she *more or less* said that. But shortly after that winter's day when I ran into her squeezing the Charmin something did happen that Roger could have told her about—with pride. Of course I don't know if he ever did, and I'd have needed to send Dez over there to find out, something I myself never did. But I doubt if he ever mentioned this incident, and it's one that I've been putting off telling you because it still fills me with a recipe for big time shame and helpless gratitude that's far inferior to one of Miss Callender's frozen pies, especially the chili con queso one.

What happened that winter of two years back complicated what happened later between Roger and me, the main subject of my story.

It's the episode that bonded me to Roger more than any other thing we ever did together. Of course, to be sure, there were others. We'd joined up to arrest and escort folks who'd broken parole restrictions. We'd interviewed people at hardware stores about shoplifters. We'd called ETS to hurry because a West Side stabbing victim was going fast—and one of them went all the way.

Those sorts of joint projects make you feel close to one another, and I'm pretty sure it was shared by the both of us. We had good work together, Roger and I. We'd generally agreed, even.

But I see I'm once more putting off telling you this tale. I'm trying to stall. It was such a mess. OK. Let's do it.

Here goes. I'm off the high diving board. Around Valentine's Day, about a year and a half before we first met Gloria Drabble, Robert Boso decided it was time to settle things between himself and his twin brother Ronny.

Robert was a screw-up from the get-go. I don't really understand how twins can be different. Don't they have the same genes or something? But then Ronny went to Beloit College, got A's in law school, got on the city council, married a judge's daughter. Robert never married; had a knack for borrowing money (some of it, according to rumors based on his brother's good name); and was even better at starting businesses that went to wrack and ruin. He always managed to worm out of debt, and I myself for one never knew how, but some people in town thought it was because some of the big shots didn't want to admit they'd been taken in by the guy.

His last failed business was a printing shop. Robert was a glad-hander; never a face without a smile. Life was always going to get better. Even now, it was great. He was tall and hirsute, and his face had so many follicles on it that when the mouth and teeth came out for their encore number, the smile was just jolting. No sun ever came behind such a bearded cloud with as much spectacle and aplomb as when Robert smiled, and yet he never went anywhere without packing his grin along. I think some people with funds in this river town just never tired of the show. It must have been mesmerizing. With Robert you just had this strong conviction that life was getting better and better and better, and never mind that he knew nothing whatsoever about printing or about burgers or whatever else he turned into hash.

There was one other little detail. Robert was also a loco and angry man. And finally one cold cloudy evening, the kind that's so cold even the low cloud cover fails as a blanket, as Robert sat in the dark of his near east side house, over mortgaged of course, which he'd managed to finance with his ex-wife's dwindling inheritance, Robert made a phone call. He made a phone call to us down at the copper shopper. He said he'd planned to kill himself and gotten Ronny over there to talk him out of it. But that, he continued, had been a ruse. By the time I got there, and by the time Roger joined me—oh, and we had four or five more uniforms hanging around, flashing their big red roofs and loosening the holsters that housed their lead just in case—I was the point guy on the phone with Robert.

"Jeremy, big guy. I'm here. I've got Ronny here. He's the golden boy. I'm the pile of pig guts, OK? The pig gut guy is going to shoot the golden boy dead, and then the pig gut guy is going to turn himself into even more pig guts, OK? And you can bury me that way, too, if you want. No pig minds dying if he can take the gold with him."

I was supposed to talk Robert Boso out of this little design. And as I tried to do so, I made a huge error. I started to feel sorry for the guy. Now they tell you in cop school, with hostage situations, to do all the right things: stay cool, don't do anything rash, see things from the nut job's point of view. And so, standing out there in the overzealous air conditioner of a Valentine's Day night, with my parka wrapped around the rolls in my pulpy abs, and waiting for Roger to arrive to help me out, I commenced to pity the guy. This is not what the book says you should do. It says you should empathize with the guy or gal but not sympathize with them.

My mind got onto this racetrack, though; a sort of Kentucky Derby of cognitive foolishness, and I began to imagine the depredations of being Robert. It wasn't just jealousy. It wasn't just that you had this beard to make you look macho while your brother was smooth-faced and deft and able to take over a room with a quiet but knowing voice and didn't need to hide behind some smiley faced Hell's Angels act. It was that you loved this twin brother. You admired him. You wanted to be like him. But he was too busy making a success of himself but stopping every now and then to help bail you out maybe, sort of like a guy walking a dog who picks up the poop but only when the neighbors are watching. You, Robert, must have been the lover, and he (Ronny) was the beloved. And the beloved found himself always embarrassed by you. I don't know why (or even if) Robert loved his twin, whether it was because he wanted to be just like him or wanted some sort of approval even though he was the black bearded ram of the family.

To tell the truth, I think these thoughts were probably off the same bill of goods as the crazy Robert's pig guts, and I even think they were projections on my part. I was a lover myself, and outside of Dez there seemed to be a tremendous dearth of lovers back. I was myself always looking on the outside at beloveds on the inside. I thought of Mary secure in her residence taking the wrappers off the paper towels and thinking more of them than she would ever think of me. Listen to me. Am I sappy or what?

"Look, Robert. You need to let me talk to Ronny. You say he's there. We need to know he's there. Otherwise, you're wasting police time, OK? We're not that big on trying to make sure you don't shoot yourself. Don't get me wrong. We'll stick around if that's the case. And I know life's been tough, OK? But don't you want to see what's going to happen tomorrow? I hear a warm front's coming. I'll take you to a Snappers game in May, all expenses paid."

There was a five second pause. Ronny Boso's voice came on the line. "Jeremy? Look, he's got his pistol. It's the one we inherited from our dad. He's holding it on me. He's already showed me it's loaded. He says he means to kill me. He says he'll kill himself. I will talk to him. He's my brother. He knows I love him. We all do. (I can imagine Robert shaking his facial armpit with eyes at this remark, and scoffing away.) But whatever happens, he gave me the phone so that I can tell you: this is serious. I'm here. Rob is mad at me. He's mad at life. He wants to kill me. He says he will. Do what you can, OK? Over and out, Jeremy, and thanks for doing all you do." Even at the point of death, Ronny managed to close with a charming remark.

Well, that settled it. We had a rather dramatic scene on our hands. We had a crazed failure of a brother who was in a hellish fury and wasn't going to take it any more and was going to bail and make sure someone important—and with a high coefficient of genetic relationship to boot—was going with him. What were we supposed to do?

Behind me I heard the muted chatter of the squad car radios. They were all buzzing about what was coming down. Every now and then I heard a sort of stupid guffaw that reminded me that whatever happened life was going to go on as dumb and invincible as ever.

Robert came back on my line. Beloit was a small enough town that he knew me a little bit. We were nodding buddies, Bobby and I. "Satisfied, Jeremy, big man? Satisfied? Now it's just a matter of time before the pig guts assembly line starts up. Could be now. Could be an hour from now. You and Ronny and the rest of you will just have to wait. For once in my life, I'm totally in charge."

"That's not true, Robert. You've been in charge lots of time. Roger Webb and I have eaten burgers you were in charge of. [maybe I shouldn't have mentioned a failed business?]. You'll be in charge tomorrow and the next day and the next month. You've had bad breaks. You owe money. We get that. But you know, Robert, you only need the one bright thing and the whole complex changes. Life, my friend, is unpredictable. You're hurting. If you end it, life won't be unpredictable. You won't have a chance to get surprised. Ronny isn't going to hold this against you. He's not going to press charges. I know that. You know that. Drop the goddamned gun. Put Ronny back on and let him tell us he's about to leave."

"Yeah, Jeremy. But you also told me my suicide wasn't that big a deal to the BPD. You only sweet talk me because you want to save Mr. Important."

"I was kidding, Robert. I just wanted to make sure Ronny was really there. Once he's out we'll stay here night and day until we know you're OK. We love you, man."

"Yeah, sure. Sure you do, Jeremy. What do you know about love anyhow?"

He had a point there. But I knew a lot about love. I thought about it a lot under my fat man funny act. I was an expert on love. It's just that I was an expert on love in the abstract. Wilma Riddlehauer was an expert on Wittgenstein. She never knew the man. So what? There are all sorts of experts.

Roger arrived. I briefed him. I called Robert back on the cell. The uniforms were still hanging around, as though they could help by driving their vehicles into the living room or something.

"We're here, Robert. We're here for you and we're here for Ronny. Look, I know it sucks to be you sometime. You said I knew nothing about love. You're right in a way. But then you and I both feel we aren't loved back, right? It's awful. But like I say, Robert, it only takes one. You're forty. You got years left. Now do me a favor. Think of the best and brightest thing in your life and imagine that that best and brightest thing is the thing that wants you to live. This is really about you living, Robert. Ronny has a lot to live for. You and I both know that. This is about you. You're the one with the power here. You're the one who will say yes or no to life. It's your life we're talking about here because what happens to your life determines what happens to Ronny. So it's you, Robert. You're the star. What's the best and brightest thing you want to live for?"

I thought of a passage we'd once read back at River City College. Yeah, Wittgenstein again. That's right, I'm a cop quoting a philosopher. But old W. himself was a hospital orderly. If Wittgenstein can be an orderly, then I can be a cop quoting a philosophical orderly. Of course I never told Robert I was quoting old Wittgenstein. I just sort of did. I said:

"Think of the warm front, Robert. Think of how much nicer it will be. Or just think about the clouds you'll see in the morning. How come these clouds came to be? How come they exist at all? Isn't that a wonderful question? Now, do me a favor. Focus on those clouds you'll see. And think: if those clouds have a reason to be, so do I. And so let's get to those clouds in the A.M., Robert, and then once we get to them let's think about breakfast and lunch and taking a walk. Want to meet my cat, Robert? There's so much, Robert. Come on, Robert."

Was I laying it on or what? But it was what I'd been taught. Tell the guy you like him. Tell him you understand. Divert him with nice thoughts. Help him take baby steps. The longer you get him to put off the evil deed the better chance you have to postpone it indefinitely.

I'd gotten so wound up with this plea that I'd forgotten how frigid it was. I could have used a warm front, but I hardly felt the chill. Counseling potential murder suicides will do that to a man, whether he's a philosopher or not or has an investigative cat or not.

As you can see above, the last thing I'd said to Robert Boso, the failed and spiteful and maybe lunatic sibling, was "Come on."

Robert did. He did come on. The two shots were booms in the icy night. They were the fire that did not warm things. They were the flames that only made things frostier. At first they were startling; then they were dreadful; then they were the explosions of despair.

They were also about fifteen seconds apart. Robert had decided that the clouds and the warm front and meeting my cat and going to watch the Snappers lose in May weren't quite enough. I wondered if it had ever been even close.

I was a little on the weepy side—not too much—when I told Roger that was it. I tried, I told Roger. I know you did, he said. I'm going on in, I said, because one or both of them might still be alive somehow.

No, said Roger, you're not. You're not going in, Jeremy. "My gut's my little pal, Jeremy. My gut tells me you shouldn't go in there. I'm listening to my little pal, Jeremy, and you're going to listen to him, too. You're upset. And you're going to stay right here and be upset with me. You're not setting even one flat foot in the direction of that house."

Roger's little pal told him to call for a SWAT team. It took them forty-five minutes to arrive. They had the full gear, the helmets and vests and assault rifles and all the menace that went therewith. I think Roger would have slugged me if I'd tried to go into Robert's house solo, or even with the useless uniforms behind me. He was right of course. In these matters you wait for SWAT. But the manual doesn't say anything about your feelings for a couple of guys whose lives you've tried to save with B.S. about the wondrous being of clouds. Forty-five minutes is a long time. You can die in forty-five minutes. But Roger wasn't going to have me doing anything other than stupidly waiting out those forty-five gruesome minutes.

And I thought Roger *was* stupid. There were two shots. Robert said he was going to kill himself and his brother. What else could those two shots mean? Robert's house was a dark gray job with one of those semi-arched roofs. It looked like some villainous eyebrow, and I swear the windows were curving in and out on me, like those shimmering bubbly black dots you're supposed to be able to see at the eye clinic if your retinas aren't shot. I think this was due to the strain of my phone calls. But it was over now. Boom.......boom had settled that. I'd failed. But maybe somewhere a heart still beat, an eye still lived that would see the morning clouds and feel the early taste of March they had on tap for us next week. I was going in, or I would have if Roger hadn't told me no way in hell and quoted the procedural manual to me. Was the book itself written by his little gutsy pal? Nah. Roger wasn't a by-the-book man. He just went by his instinct and then quoted the book in convenient support. He wasn't being logical either. But he guessed right. I was logical, played the percentages. I guessed wrong, and it would have cost me the opportunity to hear any more investigative reports from Dez.

SWAT went in; knocked down the door of Roberts' Adams Family place. And right away there was another boom and an f-word and then another boom and then a boom-boom. One of the SWAT guys had taken one in the chest, but the flak jacket turned it into a scratch. And the rest of them finished Robert off, who wasn't dead or even shot when they went in. Robert was faking us out. He wanted to take someone else with him. It could easily have been me. Is this what happens to a guy whose twin buys an Acura and pays cash while you bankrupt burgers? Later his current mistress told us she wasn't surprised. He was, she wept, pretty goddamned deranged. Wasn't it great that she finally decided to tell us?

. She just hadn't wanted to tell anybody. She was prominently seated at their double funeral, heavily attended, and stood at the graveside where Robert and Ronny were buried together in irony-rich eternity.

I'd always liked Roger. I loved his wife. He didn't know that and by this time wouldn't have much cared. That's another story. Now I *really* liked him. He'd made me look bad but was the author of my salvation, and it was Roger that made sure I'd see the clouds in the morning—actually, it was sunny, but hey, no weatherman is perfect.

Roger and I were lifers. I was sure of it then. With his gut and my head we'd go places—well, anyhow, we'd have a job in Beloit as long as we wanted it.

I loved Roger's wife. I merely liked Roger. I felt closer to Roger, of course, much closer, especially after he saved my life, even if he did make me feel dumb. Isn't that some kind of love anyhow?

What happened later is too bad for words. Words are what we have. Well, it's what I have. You probably have more. Most people do.

PART TWO:
COOKING UP FRANGO MINTS

8: Lady Godiva's Box

The Bosos were two summers back in the squad car's rearview mirror. I tried not to think about them too much. That was then. This is now. And speaking of now, Roger had a lot more on tap for me at Mac's that late summer night. He got slurrier and slurrier with every fizz times 2. He told me that if he ever had to draw his piece and fire it in genuine danger and anger he'd empty the clip. He figured he'd do a lot of missing so it's better to be safe than sorry. I was pretty sure that wasn't in the manual. Me, I have a gut so paunchy that I can't even button my suit coat. so you can sort of see the opening side of my piece whenever I moved my arms back. Sometimes I think that in the summer my piece gets sweated on so much that it won't fire anyhow—too damp. I guess it's best to conclude that neither Roger nor I had better need our weapons for more than bluff. Mine's too wet, and his is too loony.

I see I'm still talking about him in the present tense.

Finally at seven p.m. or so he said he had to face the Mary Music. He went near west side and I went far west side. Mary would be waiting for him with thoughts of intimacy. Dez would wait for me with thoughts of feeding and gossip. She was a better detective than I was, and maybe even better than Roger.

The next couple of days were quiet. Not a lot happens in Beloit by way of big crime waves, this despite the town's reputation in the state of Wisconsin as Murder City. If Beloit was in New Jersey it would be considered pastoral. But Wisconsin is a wussy state, so our occasional bar fights mean that we're a really bad-assed place. What are you going to do?

But then came Thursday of the very tail end of August. Lots began to pop. Roger and I had to look in on the Wartenburgs, Phil and Gladys, who were having their bi-annual domestic tiff, which brought complaining phone calls from neighbors. This took us over to Central Avenue in a row of tall skinny houses that looked like they'd been on a forced starvation diet. Paint chipped. Porches sagged. Phil and Gladys were retired, didn't have a lot to live on, and despised each other. Beloit isn't a dangerous town, but it does seem that it's a city where people who live together hate each other. I'm thinking the Wartenbrugs; Rose and Susan. Roger and Mary. Maybe Beloit is the Capital of Bad Roommates. Would Andy and Glory Drabble be included in that? Don't ask.

Anyhow, Roger and I shouldn't have been dealing with this domestic stuff, but at the time there were three fender-benders in town, and the boys and girls who wore identical suits were preoccupied with those.

Gladys was slatternly and her skin needed ironing but she was feisty. She said Phil had struck her because she was a lousy cook. She was on the sinking porch—I was somehow reminded of a sailor boy on a burning deck—screaming loud enough that a few corpses might have stirred over in the Oakwood Cemetery, about half a mile off. Phil was stooped and pasty with flaking skin. If he'd been a movie monster he'd be Dandruff Man. Like their house, they'd declined. He was shouting too and said he'd never done any such thing, but she *was* a lousy cook—he'd fess up to that much.

Sometimes Gladys gets so riled we need to take her to a cell to cool. That was the edition of Gladys today. She was slinging her fists and was really, truth be told, scrambled. She was a modem that needed restarting. We got her into the squad car. I fastened my coat to make sure she didn't grab my rod. I do this in emergencies.

The last thing she said as we rustled her into the back seat was, "I hate Phil with the heat of a thousand suns." I wondered how long she'd been rehearsing that one and also thought that if she had gotten that scripted, how nuts could she be? But she was acting extremely nutsy. She was really distraught. She wouldn't be a threat to others. She might be a threat to herself. We couldn't leave her there with Phil.

He protested. "Why are you taking my wife off like this?" He was frazzled and loud. The skin flakes from his face were twisting in the air like leaves when you know a tornado might be coming.

"To calm her down," said Roger.

"She is calm."

"You could have fooled me, Phil," I said.

"If you think she's crazy now you should have seen her before you got here. She's calming down right now."

"We'll give her a cup of decaf tea at the station to help her complete the work, Phil. Bye."

Phil had a point. As soon as she saw we were moving downtown—did I tell you that headquarters is practically on the

Illinois border so that we can pretend we're a little closer to Lincoln, who also called fo tranquility but rarely got it—she got pretty quiet, with infrequent whimpering the only communication for her closed mobile quarters.

Roger and I could be forgiven for thinking this would be the highlight of our working day.

We were wrong.

Rose alerted us to a phone call. She was about to buzz our cells when we walked in the door after having left Gladys with lockup. You may wonder how we could get away with arresting Gladys just because she was out of her mind. But that's called disturbing the peace. Besides, Phil, for all his protests, could use some decompression time, too. They'd be fine until maybe next spring, when the warm weather would bring their insanity out of the winter closet. The neighbors would call. Phil and Gladys had emerged from their cocoon.. They were outside again, fighting on the porch. Somebody would have to separate them. I don't know if Phil ever hit Gladys, but when there's a possibility you send somebody out. Once she truly had a black eye.

But then on that day so did Phil.

By this afternoon he'd be calling the station begging for us to bring her home.

Am I wandering, or what? You must think I'm Dez on a stealthy stroll or something. About that phone call: Rose reported that it was from a Mrs. Gloria Drabble out on Shopiere Road. She'd found something. She wanted Roger and me to come out and have a look. Rose was busy, trying to enter data and field incoming calls about a vagrant in South Beloit and explaining that we don't normally "do" South Beloit. We do well to take care of North Beloit. Otherwise, Rose would have told us all about the latest fuss with Susan. Bet on it. Anyhow, we got away in good time from her.

Fine. We'd had a productive escape from Rose. But speaking of an efficient usage of police time, why were we heading out to see Mrs. Gloria Drabble again? What had she found? Why did she want us to look at it? What could we do when we did look at it? Was it a threatening note? Somehow I doubted it was a threatening note. But I did know this: I was back in our car with Roger Webb, heading once more out to see Glorious Gloria on what seemed so much like one of those fool's errands so that, if this was not one of those, then they were like the unicorn. Or Bigfoot.

She was waiting for us, a bit enhanced this time. The pleated skirt just above the knees was gone and a gold pair of pedal pushers had taken their place, as though the loose skirt of yesteryear was an understudy for the real star or something. Her copper hair was no muss, no fuss; no don't in her 'do. She sported a refined pageboy style you only saw in movies about the 1920s, though I liked Mary's a lot better. You could call her a flapper, Good Housekeeping version. She had as much cheerful life as she ever did—that blend of Plains State optimism suffused with fretting over what might, she admitted, be a leftover from her imagination. I knew a lot about imagination, but I had Dez to help me keep mine well informed. I didn't think that plump Persian of hers had the stuff. Mrs. Drabble exuded a pained smile, as though Nebraska was trailing Kansas 14-0 but surely the Cornhuskers would catch up.

"I really thought you should see this. It makes me think this isn't all me just seeing things. You know, in the past it's been a rustle here, a shadow there. There was nothing concrete. But this is concrete. Well, it's paper, not concrete. But you see my point."

While at Beloit I'd taken a course in the philosophy of Wittgenstein, and yes, I understood from his theory of language, plus my actually speaking English, that "concrete" could mean more than "cement," whereupon Gloria Drabble presented us with the bottom of a long, six inch box. And yes, it was made of paper; cardboard to be precise.

Mrs. Drabble had on a pleasing shirt of citrine silk. The pants told us more about her shape. It was honed; I think, at the North Pointe Fitness Center, a tony place in nearby Roscoe. Not for Mrs. Drabble the decline of the early middle-aged body. She moved quickly, almost jerked as she walked even a short distance. Her bottom was a bit saggy, but everything else was fit. She was slim with just enough hip to make it all interesting. Above all, she was positive—not in the sense of being certain but in the sense of being optimistic. Her ivory brick suburban ranch could be burning down and she'd still say that at least it hadn't exploded yet, and maybe one of the smaller glass IKEA tables could be saved before it melted down into Windex or something. She apologized for troubling us but at the same time assured us that everything was going to be all right. "Chipper" would be the right word for her.

I wondered why Mr. Andrew Drabble had seemingly cast her off. Any man prone to depression would find her uplifting, right? But maybe he wasn't the depressed type. Maybe he thought all that bubbling was fake. Who understands marriage? I'd need Dez to do a little spying to get this one

There was no label on the box bottom. The top was missing. It was longish. Roger and I took it and looked at it. He passed it to me. "Where'd you find this," he asked.

"By the bedroom window just this morning. I was walking over there to turn the hose on. I wondered if I should call you. I decided I should."

"Mrs. Drabble, do you mean *the* bedroom window where you think this prowler was?" I asked this question more as a plaint than anything else, because if she said no, her illogic and time wasting would have depressed *me*. Please say yes, I thought.

"Yes. I found it by that very window."

"Have you heard other noises?"

"In truth, no. But then I found this box bottom."

"Have you ever seen this sort of thing before?" Roger was doing it all quite right, by the book, but somehow I didn't think they were thinking of Gloria Drabble when they wrote that book. The question was: what book did they write when thinking of Mrs. Gloria Drabble?

"Yes. I even think I know what it is. It's the bottom of a Lady Godiva Chocolate box. The top has the label on it."

"How many chocolate pieces can you get into this thing?" I'm sure she thought that this was just the sort of thing The Portly One would ask. But as usual she was hyper-pleasant about it.

"Six, Officer Dropsky. Six birthday chocolates."

"You've been given this on your birthday, "asked Roger, "or you've given it on your birthday? Where would you get this sort of gift? Online?"

"Online, yes, though there are couple of places in Rockford that carry it. And yes, I've gotten this for my birthday. Andrew has given it to me two or three times. I've told him—watching the girlish figure and all that—but he always takes three or four of them for himself. He never gains an ounce. And they are marvelous to taste."

"Did you have a box of these in your house here?"

"No. And my birthday is in February. I think I last got one of these gifts from Andrew shortly before we split up."

Here I had an interior tantrum of silent perplexity. I mean, the contrast was slaying me. These two share chocolates to die for, and then they shed bitter tears and separate. Do you like salt liquid with those Godivas? And when Andrew moved out, did Gloria insist that he "have a nice life?" This was the sort of thing that a woman who, in Roger's words, "had a lot of life in her" might well say. Maybe decorum under pressure wasn't Mrs. Drabble's long suit, but then she wore pedal pushers, not suits.

Now for a while I had been a college boy, and now I sort of wished I hadn't been because my sense of what made sense had maybe been ruined. My standards were too high for this up-with-people housewife on Shopiere Road, east Beloit. Or maybe I just wished I'd stayed in college so I wouldn't have to deal with this massive confusion. But I tried to get to the point. Roger had gone deaf and dumb on me.

"Are you saying that your husband left this box bottom by the window and that he's the one who's been bothering you?"

She smiled reassuringly. "I think so, Officer Dropsky. I can't explain this thing any other way."

I could explain it other ways. I could imagine that the box held roach traps rather than chocolates and that as a result of some sort of hitherto unknown atomic fallout giant roaches had developed along Turtle Creek and evolved an affinity for perky early middle-aged housewives and liked to eavesdrop on them; and that they had left the bottom of the roach traps box as though to say, "You can't stop us that way."

But I said nothing for several seconds. Roger seemed lost in thought. Maybe he was pretending that Mrs. Drabble *was* Lady Godiva (forget the chocolate part), about to mount in the buff a nearby stallion just for him. Your guess was as good as mine.

9: *The Sense in Nonsense*

Roger and I said little about Gloria Drabble's alleged Lady Godiva box as we drove back to the station. Between Phil and Gladys and Gloria and Godiva it had been a hectic day. We had of course agreed to take the box bottom and even put it in a plastic evidence sleeve. And Roger and I never formally agreed not to talk about what we'd experienced. We just sensed that it wasn't a good idea. We knew each other. We were professionals. Hell, even Sherlock Holmes said it was a capital mistake to draw conclusions in advance of full data, and Old Sherlock had never even had to set foot in Beloit in order to attain such wisdom.

So we kept quiet. We arrived at headquarters. We went our different ways, I first to the Stop n' Go, where I knew I could find some of the frozen tater tots I craved, and which would be eminently microwavable, right? And while there who should I run into but Wilma Riddlehauer? She was one of my old professors at Beloit, about fiftyish and a fine philosophy teacher.

She was paying for her gas. No fattening foods for Wilma, who was also a vegan.

"There you are, Jeremy. What's going on? When are you going to come back to Beloit?"

I thought I had never left Beloit, but I knew what she meant. "Around the thirteenth of Never, Professor. It's good to see you, though."

"I'm offering a Wittgenstein seminar this fall. You should sit in. You made a lot of sense about him, and not every undergrad philosophy student can say that. So how's policing?"

"Thanks for the offer. I think I'd be in the way. As for policing, well, it's making less sense all the time."

"You recall, though, what Larry (as you once called him) Wittgenstein said about sense and nonsense: that in the right context all nonsense can become sense. Well, that's what the later Larry said. And you'll remember that the later Larry disagreed with the earlier one."

I did recall that. Professor Riddlehauer looked good. The salt and pepper hair flowed in good health, as though it were hearty seasoning rather than a sign of age. She still had that little stoop that made her look bowed down and humiliated, but that was just posture, and she certainly didn't act humiliated. Here was someone who loved her job and was put on earth to do it. You might not be able to say that about one Jeremy Dropsky, Esquire.

Doctor Wilma smiled in a radiantly lop-sided way. This was my cue. It was my turn to say something, but what? Suddenly, I had it!

"That must be what I'm missing in cop work: the right context."

"You'll find it. You're bright, Jeremy. I'm glad you're with the police. Think about that seminar, however."

I said I would, and she trundled off to her car and I bumbled on to the frozen food pantry.

And I thought: The Lady Godiva Chocolates Box makes no sense. That worried me. But there was an even greater fear: that I would go to work tomorrow morning, barely avoid Rose's creepy laments about poor sad Susan, and find that to Roger the whole thing made perfect sense. It's not easy for a man to conclude that his partner is either a genius or a madman, even if that same man's partner once kept him from walking into the valley of death.

The tater tots were good, scrumptious even. Dez asked if she could have a few pieces or five or six of them, and I obliged with three. You have to keep your sources happy. She'd had an industrious day. The cat door is always open, rain or shine or hail or ice. She leaped over and then around a few sticks of cast-off furniture, and sat on the floor beneath me. She had a lot to tell.

At this point some of you are thinking that it's not Roger but me who's the crazy one. I am not. Dez tells me nothing that I've not already figured out for myself. No, check that. It's when I see Dez that I *realize* what I've already figured out. She's my inspiration. I *know*—I'm not a nutball—that Rose and Susan live three miles from here in an apartment out on Prairie Avenue near the hospital and south of Telfer Park. And I know they have an interior unit, so I know that Dez can't possibly perch herself by their window and find out anything. And I know that even Dez can't go three miles and back in a single day. I know all that. But hey, Dez is, like, my fellow-feeling. She's my sense of drama. She's the muse, sort of, of my social imagination. When I think of

Dez watching Roger and Mary and Susan and Rose, I just know what's going down, OK?

And now Dez was nuzzling my left foot.

And she's watching Rose and Susan seething at home out on Prairie.

And Rose is spread out on her bed, dominating it, and reading a romance novel, a heart-pounding book with a bare chested swashbuckler on the cover and a buxom tight-corseted brunette facing him with a look of both alarm and desire on her glamorous face. And in the book they will play a game over about two hundred fifty pages in which they will go from seeming indifference to one another to a climactic scene in which he both rescues her from rape and almost rapes her himself in the melee. And it will not be easy to get into all her late Renaissance cloth in order for him to take possession of that prized bodice. But it will happen, and they will get married, as duke and duchess or something, and live happily ever after while nearly re-enacting the same rescue scene every night just so that he can keep feeling like a saving hero and she can keep feeling like the beloved saved one. Oh, and the intervening duke on the cover will likely look a lot like the very imposing Roger.

And Rose will read this one and then another one, which she can get off the book stall at Shopko's on Prairie Avenue, just down the street from her place, and she will know that this will never happen to her but she will continue to wish that it would and be bitter that it has not and be sure that it would if only she didn't have the abiding burden of the crippled Susan.

And Susan will be in the other bedroom. She too will be propped up, and her withered and useless legs will be conveniently hidden from her, and she too will be reading—but a magazine, not a novel. And this too will have come from Shopko, on the lower rack so that she can reach it. Susan is, or once was, a pretty woman with an aquiline face and long brown hair, but the face was pinched from anger at her rotten luck and then, proving that for every action there's a reaction, it fell into sagging disarray, somewhat like a dog's droopy tail, which shows that when a dog's tail does not wag it must do something much less interesting and inspiring. And so Susan frowns, her face like the disarray of spilt syrup, and she goes over a magazine article on why some women are cruel to other women. And the article states that the ones who are cruel are moral idiots, and this to a tee describes Rose, whom she has long given up asking for assistance in helping her get into bed. She'd rather fall and ding her elbow than ask that fat bitch for help.

All this Dez reports to me. She's a cutie, and I am pleased and honored to be associated with a peppy and lovely feline that revels in her freedom and not in the misery of two unhappy women, one obese and the other immobile, on the north side of Beloit, or in the sufferings of my poorly-married partner who likely has some strange ideas about a purported Lady Godiva Box Bottom.

10: The Evidence of No Evidence

The next day down at the River City Constabulary was pretty uneventful on the surface of the annals of crime. A high school kid got his wallet and ring lifted by a mugger, who seemed to have nothing to do with the high school. The kid had wandered a bit too far from campus during lunch break in order to sneak a cigarette, he said, but probably to sneak a joint. There was a burglary on Prairie Avenue near the old K-Mart. It was in one of those down-in-the-heels ranch style houses that dentists used to live in but that realtors occupied now, and Beloit had a real estate market cooler than lukewarm.

Rose made a few cracks about Susan, but nothing special. It was something like, "I'm doing well for somebody living with a crippled ingrate," though maybe I'm making this more eloquent than it was. Or maybe she said "inmate."

All of this was pretty unremarkable, but then came something more important. I had to discuss the box bottom with Sergeant Roger Webb—or, more to the point, what we were going to do by way of follow up.

We went to Hansen's for a burger and brew. It's on the river and has tasty food and once upon a time a menu noted for its artful misspelling. It was kind of cute as long as the burgers and mushrooms were good. They got rid of the funny spelling with no negative effects on the food. It was still more than OK. Roger and I sat at one of the high tables.

"I'll come to the point, Rog. I see no evidentiary value in that thing. There might be value of course if we checked it for prints or ran a DNA on it. But we won't. We can't."

Roger shook his head in manic agreement, one of those jack in the box nods. This seemed odd. Why all the pep? "You're right. And if we did run prints or DNA we'd find maybe his and hers, and he would say so what because after all he once gave her a box of chocolates and she could have planted it on the property and tried to incriminate him."

Was Roger celebrating this scheme? He seemed happy.

I decided to ignore that. "Well, I'll disagree with you a little bit there, Sergeant. If we found his prints and his DNA on the box— but not hers—that would implicate him. But then first of all, I believe the house is partly in his name. What's wrong with him going onto his own property?"

This seemed to put a brake on Roger's curious joy. "I hadn't though of that angle. Hell, Jeremy, you're right about that."

"I'm not a failed college kid for nothing."

"No, you are not. But hey, this is all…what do you failed college kids call it—academic? There are no grounds to run prints or DNA either one on this thing. Nobody's been threatened, right?"

"The whole thing is a phantom. I'll be honest with you, Roger. I'm not sure why we're spending so much time on this. Is it because she lives in Turtle Creek and her husband is an ex-Beloiter who used to be a big builder around here? Yet he's the one she wants us to suspect as the bad guy. I don't get it."

"Well, I'd say it's because, well, when the first call came up all the folks in dark blue were busy, and we handled it, and she's just asked for us since then. Am I right?"

"That must be it. Could be something else, too. Could be that even though they like to call us detectives, a lot of of the stuff we investigate is clear-cut. We don't know where a bad guy is, but we know who he is. I'd almost say that this Gloria thing is, like, a mystery. But I'd say it's a pretty flimsy mystery. It's like Rose's resentment of Susan: pretty thin soup, even if it does give her a reason for getting up in the morning—besides, you know, wanting to make enough money to eat Frosted Flakes."

"She's a bit of a Tony the Tiger herself, except that Tony's a lot nicer person."

I thought this pretty witty of Roger. He was in an excellent mood. Was this because he and Mary were getting it on again or because he felt relieved not to have to do anything about Lady Godiva's Box—or what? But then he threw me a forkball.

"Anyhow, this box does give us a reason to have a chat with Andrew Drabble."

"What?"

"Well, it would be routine. We'd just check in and say that his wife has been reporting a prowler and that the prowler might have left this box bottom and has he ever seen anything like this before?"

"You're not planning on putting the heat on him?"

"Of course not. What sort of bad cop do you think I am? Don't answer that. It would be just a routine call. He needs to know about Mrs. Drabble's troubles from an official source, and if he is involved, he needs to know that official sources are sort of on the case. That would warn him off."

Even I had to admit this had some logic. "But," I said, "we need to let Rockford know we're coming to call."

"Of course. That's standard courtesy. And when we see Mr. Drabble we'll emphasize this is strictly routine."

So this was why Roger was so happy. He was happy because the box could yield no forensic evidence, so that meant he could get a free, all-expenses-paid trip to Rockford, Illinois. That's what I thought anyhow. And this whole time I thought it was because he and the alluring Mary had had great sex followed by a close emotional interaction in which two souls joined as though super glued.

I know I don't get marriage. I wonder sometimes if I get policing either.

11: Dez Takes on Door Hinges

Roger and I agreed that we'd take a little drive down to Drabble, Inc. the following day or the one after that. We'd take Lady Godiva's (alleged) Box Bottom with us and do a very low-level confrontation with the Master Builder. If you're like me, you already know that "Box Bottom" sounds off-color. I tried to ignore this. I tried to look forward to a date with Marie Callender's extra large turkey potpie: just what my waistline needs. I avoided the beef because beef comes from mammals and Dez is a mammal and I have to honor Dez, who is my eyes and ears. I wished I could send her to Rockford to spy on Andrew Drabble so that we could eliminate him as a suspect in what was likely not a crime to start with. But so far Rockford was beyond her territory.

She'd padded through the garage cat door and awaited her nightly ration of Kitty Sensations wet and dry mix. Between hearty bites she told me about her visit to Professor Wilma Riddlehauer's seminar on Wittgenstein. This was pretty amazing of Dez, not only because the seminar hadn't started yet—Dez time travels, as do most undersized orange female tabbies—but also because for a cat Dez is quite good at reporting philosophical argument. She sneaked into the World Affairs Center on campus where the class was being held and waited outside the door that Wilma R. always left open when she taught. And so Dez told me that Dr. Riddlehauer, stooped with wet stringy long gray white hair (it had just rained) and with wire rim glasses strung across her long neck, lest the absent-minded professor forget them, had stated the following with ferocious intensity and precision:

If you need to put Wittgenstein into a philosophical category, you might say he was a specialist in logic. He himself said he was not a philosopher but a killer of philosophy, but he also seems to indicate that he is a philosopher who is out to get rid of traditional philosophy. You can take your pick. I say he is a philosopher whose special expertise was logic.

I want to treat him that way today—because he made a logical distinction between what I'll call "hinge" propositions and "door" propositions. Take a board. It doesn't become a door until you put it on hinges so that it can swing and let you in or out. Whether the board is a door hinges on a hinge. Now once you can establish that it is a door, you can talk about whether it's a good door or a white door or a long door or a French door or whatever. And so we take up the problem Wittgenstein took up in one of his last efforts—whether or not you can or can't say that this is my hand and that it is not only my hand (and nobody else's) but it also exists—and Wittgenstein argued that this statement is a hinge proposition. Unless we can state this as certain, we can't, for example, look at a hand to see if it's broken or big or little or white or dead or anything else. So what does a hinge proposition do? It makes possible all sorts of inspections: of white doors or broken hands, or yellow doors or big hands. That the hand exists is the hinge proposition; that it's big is the door proposition—but you can't have the door without the hinge.

A stout boy in the back of the class raised his hand. *Yes, Jeremy,* said Dr. Riddlehauer.

Suppose I think I have half of a box—the bottom half, by which I mean a cardboard tray about six inches long, with about an inch of cardboard surrounding the bottom. Can I say for sure that this is the bottom of a cardboard box? Might it not be something else? Might it not just be a cardboard tray that you can put little rocks on? I mean, who says that it's the bottom half of a box? Can I say that for sure? Is that a hinge proposition or not?

I think we should talk about this after class, Jeremy. You've raised a complicated point. I'd say, though, that without all of the box there you can't say for sure that this is the bottom half of one.

Dez finished her report. She smacked her mouth, a sign that she was full, and hopped onto my porky lap and purred. I petted her and liked her nuzzling her nose back and forth on my plump white hand. She was my Mary, or what I had instead. I thought of Roger's plan to visit local mogul Andrew Drabble. I didn't think it was necessary, but I couldn't really see anything wrong with it either, as long as we had the time, and we had only one possibly big case pending. I still didn't see why Roger should be so glad of the trip south.

I couldn't figure it out—not then. Besides, that night I was too exultant about Dez's report: that a Beloit College professor might someday help me figure out whether the bottom of a box proved that it once held Godiva's best dark chocolates.

As Dez began to knead my tummy she seemed to say, *Aren't you glad that the thing you serve my kitty-wet on doesn't require a top, so we have the whole thing and don't ever need to doubt that it is a dish?*

12: Gas Grills and Cough Syrup

Say what you will about Charlie Baxter, chief of detectives, but the guy always stands up straight. It's like he's waiting for his statue and doesn't want to die first and so he just stands there like a pillar and expects the hot bronze to be poured over him and expects somehow to survive. He called us in first thing next morning. I think he'd been so forceful about the order that when Rose passed it on, she didn't even have the time, or nerve, to tell us about how Susan was plotting to stampede her at fifteen miles per hour with her chair.

Charlie's posture was impeccable. His white shirts were not. They were always wrinkled. His suit coat had a sheen that spoke of old age. His face sagged, as though the spine and the visage were in some sort of tension with each other, but it was hard to tell which was holding up the other. I wondered for a second if Andrew Drabble, who supposedly knew a thing or two about construction, would approve of this plan.

Charlie said he'd read the memo on the Gloria Drabble business and this morning had just gotten Roger's report that he and I, after spending some time with the estranged Missus, would be calling on the wealthy and successful Mister. Charlie didn't nix that, but he complicated it. We weren't surprised by what he said next. I knew we had a big case pending, but we didn't know how pending it would turn out to be.

"You can visit Rockford if you think it's needed as long as you notify Rockford police down there. But don't think you have to rush, guys. In fact, you don't have to rush to Rockford. It gets even better. You aren't even allowed to rush to Rockford. The thing about 'the house' is looking better than ever, or worse than ever. Perkins and Flack, the squad guys looking into it, are ready for a raid. You two will lead it. You'll supervise any evidence gathering. You'll make the arrests—that is, if there is any evidence and there are any warranted detentions. I think there will be some—both in fact."

"The house" referred to reports we'd been getting for about a week about a hole near Oakwood Cemetery. The corpses were in better shape than the house was, an almost shack with peeling teal-green paint. It was sort of stuffed a long way from the curb, as though it was the sort of bad sheep relative you'd want to shove into a drawer. It had dirty and obscure written all over its falling down front porch, which, when we drove by, made even Charlie's face look like it was standing at attention.

"OK," said this self-same Captain Baxter, "here's what we got just in the last three days. There's been a pretty good stakeout ever since the neighbors said they were having a little difficulty with their sinuses. These solid citizens got a little tired of waking up with a burn in their nostrils. They called us. We've been watching: well, Perkins and Flack have."

"Let's have it," said Roger.

"And have it you shall. Get ready."

"Sounds like a couple of Happy Meals to me," I said. I wondered if at my size I should have pushed the food analogy.

"Here it is. There's a man and woman, or you can call them a boy and a girl if you like. They're young. I think I may even know them from the description. The girl is in and out a lot. She carries garbage bags full of something heavy several times a day. Drives up in the old jalopy and hauls them into the house. Flack watched her buy seventeen bottles of cough syrup from three different drug stores over two days' time. Perkins went next door and observed a propane tank in the backyard that could double as an Olympic swimming pool if it could hold some water. If we don't find flasks and beakers inside you can kiss my family valuables. But here's the thing: we're still waiting for a warrant, and there ain't no warrant that we're gonna get one."

"When will we know?"

"The D.A. has asked by ten this morning. No Rockford vacations for you guys until we hear. It'll be, oh, 90 minutes from now. But if this house thing works out you can spend the week in Rockford if you want. That'll be your reward. Give my best to the clock collection and the Jap gardens."

"The clocks are no longer there, Captain."

"OK, Dropsky. Then enjoy the gardens, and don't tell me, college boy, that 'Japs' is politically incorrect."

"Japs is politically incorrect." This was Roger, who'd had no college. Roger had been strange of late. It was good to see he was still funny, or trying to be.

Was he getting on better with Mary? But that would mean she would never marry me. She would never marry me anyhow.

So absent the warrant we had nothing to do for an hour and a half. We drank coffee in our cubicles and caught up on paper work. Rose yelled at us—she wasn't far away—that she wanted to report a crime. We yelled right back and told her to call Crimestoppers.

Police headquarters in Beloit were part of a potpourri of government offices: one big, recessed, red brick building; three stories high; looming like a linebacker near the Illinois border as though it might want to change its mind about which state; and a place where you could pay your taxes and be jailed for tax evasion, all under the same slate roof. But we had had only one case of tax evasion, and that was for a Nebraska man on the run who'd speeded in Beloit, and the computer pegged him when we stopped him and he ended up a guest of Beloit City Government while the Feds from Chicago arrived. He'd been evading for ten years and got caught laundering dirty Omaha dollars in the Virgin Islands. This was all pretty exotic stuff for a good old river town like ours.

Finally word came down from On High, a.k.a. Judge Fowler, and the answer was no. We needed more than cough syrup and gas grills to get a warrant. But Captain Baxter was an ingenious fellow. He radioed Perkins and Flack to knock on the door with a fake inquiry about burglars. They did, and twenty minutes later they reported a god-awful ammonia smell and a little smoke careening around the door of one of the back rooms. Baxter conveyed this data to the D.A. who conveyed it to Judge Fowler, and by noon we had our warrant.

The trip to Captain Baxter's Jap garden had to be postponed.

13: Julie & Jim

I know it won't do for me to take stock of my life too often. It consists professionally of Roger and me visiting other people's homes and offices, and privately of me visiting my own home, where sometimes I feel more like an intruder than Dez does. She seems to be the only one truly at home there. It also occurs to me that most of the people whose homes I visit as a cop live with someone else, which I don't. Gloria Drabble is the main exception lately, but even she had Andrew for a long while, plus of course that grotesque Persian cat.

And sometimes when we visit these homes we can smell whatever is cooking. They often use stoves, these various leads and suspects, and you can smell the steak and bread. I use a microwave, and you can smell Marie's macaroni only after it first emerges. Visiting and cooking, mobility and ingestion: that's my life.

But don't feel sorry for me. Some got it worse, and among these must be the dandy couple we called upon over near Oakwood Cemetery, the guy and gal who couldn't seem to get enough big Energizer Bunnies or Liquid Vicks Vapor. The cop shows always show the search warrant intrusions to be melodramatic—you know, the bad white snow flushed down the toilet just before the police get their first knock on the door; or maybe the perp's refusal to open the door and here comes the battering ram and the Glocks drawn. The cops on these shows are always darting their two-handed rods into this corner and that one to see if something emerges that they can trigger. Or sometimes the TV police find loads of illegal immigrants that don't speak English, and this lends a kind of pathos or something to the vital search for law and order.

But most search warrant visits in Beloit don't go like that at all. This one was no exception. I gotta say, though, that this time the culprits were pretty dumb even by upper Midwestern standards. They were like a couple of kids who arranged to have their pa killed and then showed up fifteen minutes later with time cards and flashed them in the cops' faces with, "I didn't do it. Here's proof." This means: they were in on it, and in a couple of days they'll admit it. When we knocked on the door of the shanty near Oakwood, the two inside hardly came to the door (to be exact, they didn't bother to come at all but just said *yeah*), but they were sitting on a well-sprung purple couch with foam protruding and smoking, respectively, a cigarette (she) and a joint (he). They didn't say, "come in" or "welcome." They looked fried-faced straight ahead—"without affect," as I learned in one of my psych classes at Beloit College—and let us have the run of the place.

There was Roger and me and four uniforms. Yeah, we had our guns drawn but only for about ten seconds. There was no one to shoot here. They'd already shot themselves. I'd mentioned cooking a little while ago. Here there was no steak and bread in the oven. But there were plenty of pots on the stove, and they smelt every bit like the stuff boys and girls put into their organic systems in order to feel better. You had your boiling lithium and your steaming Sudafed, or whatever that stuff is they put in Sudafed. I mean if you have manic-depression and a runny nose combined, or you just want to get much higher than Ben Franklin's electric kite, then this is the place for you—the very place.

We *good* boys were pretty high ourselves. For us, excitement is spelled M-E-T-H. And yeah, we knew the lovers on the sofa. They were a couple of formerly rich kids in Beloit, Wisconsin: James Barbee and Julie Mallow. They came from an area we call "east of Milwaukee Road," on Emerson Street down into the rich-bitch area of town. This is where what was once Old Money lived, before they started putting up the McMansions out off Shopiere and along Cranston. But Turtle Creek was the key. Even the Emerson Street crowd wanted to be near the creek. You might say Turtle Crick is what Beloit has for Lake Superior or the North Atlantic. It's probably what we deserve, too. Don't get me wrong. It's pretty.

I called Jim and Julia "formerly" rich kids, but that's not really true, is it? They still are rich kids. It's just that this time they may have to wait post-slammer in order to inherit anything. The Barbees and Mallows are ancient wealth around here—the parents got all moneyed up on a glass factory that used to be here, and a tool factory that used to be here. They both got swallowed up by (a.k.a. merged with) great big whales. And they were both good makers of moolah in their day, and the kids grew up pampered by moms and dads too permissive, with booze and discipline alike, to care much for anything except when the next trip to Acapulco in

January was scheduled. For that matter, how about a little Nice in May?

Jim and Julie skipped over the local high school and went to a nearby country day outfit where they learned how to fail with grand indifference to their fate. The thing about rich kids is that they don't feel accountable. But in time J&J, who had become best friends and then, as I understand it, briefly lovers, got into stuff, and the only way they could pay their way out was, apparently, to sell it for others, bad and sometimes sad people who didn't care if their parents once made a beer bottle or an oversized drill by the tens of thousands.

We'd run them in for dealing several times, but lawyers got them a deal. This time it would go down different. Cooking meth—and they were too stoned to disguise it, I guess—is harder to bargain out, even if the gargantuan gas grill in the back yard had temporarily banked its fires and counted as no evidence at all.

I wasn't looking forward to interrogating them, and neither, I assumed, was Roger. They'd get smartass when they got the badass stuff flushed out of their systems. They'd lawyer up sky high, at least by local standards. But there was little need to put the squeeze on them, you'd think, since we had them dead even to their Miranda rights. What were they going to say? "We thought this stuff was really steak and bread. That's what happens to a couple of wealthy brats like us when we get above and over the usual drug rainbow." They could say that. No competent jury would believe them. This time they were going to become all expense paid invitees of the majestic state of Wisconsin, which continues to concede the proposition that Beloit, though almost in Illinois, is still legally a part of the Badger State.

As for Julie and Jim, they probably had no idea whether they were in Wisconsin *or* Illinois. They were in unfit condition to talk, but we still had to talk to them right away. That's what the book says, and the book never lies, well, not on purpose. A crowd had gathered in front of their broken down rental, attracted by the cop cars, and pretty soon some county forensic guys followed, and the whole lab was getting the once over and then the thrice over. Someone said it looked like they'd been cooking for about a month. Who for?

We had to give them a chance to call lawyers, and this was delicate because we weren't sure, given their residence in the twilight zip code, with their faces scrunched up and their eyes wild and frozen at once, if they understood what this was all about. Roger said he was surprised that they hadn't blown themselves to subatomic particles cooking meth, but I guessed that they'd learned to function stoned, and when we arrived they were just taking a break. The beakers were foaming like something out of Monterey Bay, though I've never actually seen Monterey Bay, so what do I know? Maybe I should send Dez out of there for a full report.

"Mr. Barbee. Ms. Mallow. You're allowed a phone call each. You reach someone, and they can call someone else on your behalf. What will it be? Do you understand me?"

A nodding of the sullen variety registered assent. Rose had to dial for them, but both calls went to Mother and Father, who had paid all the bills while J&J had had all the fun tossing their lives away with all four of their good-and-well-stoned hands.

Rose conveyed the news. The families were sending lawyers. We shouldn't try to talk to Jim and Julia until they arrived. They would be coming out of Janesville. We had to wait. When they arrived—we knew them as courteous guys who didn't like this any better than we did but were on constant family retainer—we showed them the snaps of the meth house. We showed them images of J&J on the couch. We showed them records of a rental agreement. Julie and Jimmy Boy were actually living there. They weren't just babysitting batteries. We showed the attorneys the written records of neighbors' complaints about smells. The lawyers, Carton and Westworth (from the same firm) nodded their heads—the only thing about them not dapper. They knew it would be plea bargain time, not exoneration time. The kids might make bail, but they were going to serve time.

The lawyers weren't exactly our foes. We were glad to have them sit in. We didn't want this thrown out on bad procedures. They could advise their clients not to answer. That was fine. It would be a labor saving device for Roger and me. The evidence was as overbearing as a Mack truck twenty over the limit.

The six of us settled into Room A. All of these rooms are small. They have cinder block walls. They're cramped with a little table that looks like it's recovering from a bad case of acne, along with rickety chairs. There's only official room for four. If lawyers join us, we got to bring in folding chairs for them. I sit close to the table to hide my gut. Roger sits back with his legs on tiptoes as though he's readying himself to pounce.

I like these little chats with felons because I can show off my jaunty cop routine, suffused with plenty of hard-ass cynicism and suspicion. It's a great way to mask the fact that I'm actually a lonesome, unhappy soft-ass. Roger is different. He doesn't joke. He's quiet and earnest, but you can hear the bloodhound growl beneath the mumble. He takes this job more seriously than I do. It's all he's got. Or at least that's what I once thought. He's got Mary but doesn't want her. I've got a woulda-shoulda life that gives me endless subject matter for contemplation. Besides, I get along better with Dez than he does with Mary. And Mary doesn't help him with the detective work. She's actually sort of against the detective work. Dez likes being an investigator.

"So J&J, we meet again. Last time we saw you two you were selling to eighth graders in Clinton, that hot-totting town. Now you've graduated."

"What do you mean?" This was Jim, whose dead eyes suddenly flared with anger. The young man lives—miracles will never cease.

"I mean you've gone from dealing grass to cooking meth. We might say you've gone from server to chef, right?"

I enjoyed my own humor. Nobody else was. Somebody had to. It was a nasty job. Somebody had to do it.

"We've got you guys with red paint on your hands." This was Roger, taciturn and growly, going in for the big kill, right?

"I don't plan to say anything, boys, so don't strain your ears." This was fluting Julie, who sounded like a tough nine year old and added, "The lawyers come from my parents. They'll back me up on this." She was zoned. She sounded like the automatic lady voice that leaves you a message that you have overdue library books, except that hers was more high-pitched.

"In truth, Julia, I think you have a lawyer hired by your parents and Jim has one hired by his parents. Now I don't know what your parents think of you two. You had all the privileges, as we used to say. Maybe you think lawyers hired by wealthy mom and pop types can make lithium strips and test tubes and ammonia smells go away. You're both probably out of it enough to think that. We're only talking to you now because we have to. Your lawyers have said we could. Maybe they think you're better off talking to us stoned so that later you can say you weren't in your right minds."

Westworth looked at me peripherally. I could swear he grinned. There wasn't much he could do for two wayward lost causes other than to tell these two little rich waifs to put a stopper on their pie holes.

I continued. "But we do have some curiosity about you two. Your folks probably want to know whether or not they can get their money back from the maternity ward. We want something different. We wonder if you're doing a mom-and-pop, or working for somebody else. By the way, storing the crystals in big empty cat litter containers is an original touch. Those plastic handles are dandy for lifting, aren't they? Don't you just love them? Who's coming to pick that up, Elvis Impersonators?"

"Ha, ha," stated Jim Barbee in terms of a snarl so certain they'd make Wittgenstein's thing about the hand seem ambiguous. I'll say this for the two of them. Neither looked the part of a couple of rich kids on the lam. They were both skin and bones, malnourished almost for somebody whose parents dined out on caviar enchiladas every winter. But they weren't misers with the follicles. Jim's hair hadn't been cut for so long he looked like a weeping willow shrouding an almond face. Julie's strings were halfway down her ass. They both wore wire rims. They were the druggie generation version of that painting by Grant Wood of the two Iowa farmers. I think it's in Chicago somewhere.

"Do you have anything to say in response to Sergeant Dropsky's question? Are you working alone? If you have a name you could get reduced time. I can't promise that. Up to the D.A. But it's been known to happen. How about a name?"

Julie couldn't resist this temptation. "You want us to name Mr. Big, Roger?"

"I don't think that's his name, young lady." I had to chortle inside at this. Here's Roger, an almost drunk in an estranged marriage, going all parental on this strung out doll of privilege. It goes to show, I guess, that even heavy drinkers can always find somebody to be respectable around, especially if you're a cop.

"You've broken the code, Roger. That isn't his name...if he exists. I'm not talking anymore. I don't have to, do I Mr. Carton."

"You don't. And I think you're doing well to say as little as possible. Don't do these gentlemen's jobs for them."

"I like how you call him Mr. Carton, Julie. At least you respect those who are trying to save your ass. I think we're not quite ready for truth time. You two need to get happy with the idea that you're going to be blowing out birthday candles at least three times in the mess hall of the pen. You'll be getting postcards from Mexican haciendas at General Delivery, Waupun State Prison. Then, just maybe, Mr. Big will acquire a name, though I doubt if he exists. You two seem like real entrepreneurs. Should there be a Mr. Big, you'd likely be doing this much more professionally, by which I mean deceitfully. You two are smelly and sloppy, which is why you got caught. But if Mr. Big isn't Big Foot, you can probably have a couple of extra merry birthdays on the outside if your information leads to him. I'm sure he's got his ways to get even, though. I might even tell you not to name him at all. But that's the job of your lawyers, not the work of Sergeant Webb and myself. They'll pay us just the same whatever. But I'll close like this: If you do have a Mr. Big we can get him off the streets for you well before your big homecoming on Emerson Street. Besides, I hear Acapulco has a great witness protection program."

14: My Brother the Haitian

That session went as a fifth grader might have predicted. The demonic duo lawyered up, thanks to their well-to-do parental system. They weren't especially alert but knew enough to keep mostly silent and slightly smart-ass. They were stupid in what they did, and this probably meant that they were working for no one other than themselves. If you went to their computers you'd probably find lots of Google hits on "how to open a meth brewery in your neighborhood." We'd of course have to use street sources in order to find out who was buying from them, but that wouldn't be too hard. The ones who do coke are always happy to turn in the ones who do meth because they think we'll stay away from the cokeheads for a while. It's all in a dull day's work here in River City, Wisconsin-Illinois, the only place on Planet Earth where Lincoln is a Badger.

I got home late to find Dez awaiting her grub. The cat door in the undersized attached garage was infallible. I decided to buy a place with a puny garage so that something about me, besides Dez herself, would be small. Dez and I chowed down, she from the can and I from the microwave.

I wished I'd known about Jim and Julie's Methopolis sooner, but I would never have seen Dez over there to scout it out. I don't want her nostrils burning warped and red. Besides, I don't really need Dez to imagine what's going on. She might help me to figure out other relationships, such as Susan and Rose and Roger and Mary and all the other lucky people in my life who don't have to go home to some mammal other than a cat. But I could pretty well composite Julia and James on my own—no feline assistance required, thank you very much. They wouldn't talk much over at that slatternly rental of theirs by Oakwood Graveyard. But this wouldn't be respect for the dead. They'd just be busy cooking, sometimes with the scenic gas grill. They'd spend a lot of time on their phones or tablets. They'd have music blaring. They'd snort up and maybe shoot up from time to time. They'd be just two old friends giving each other permission to ruin themselves in short-term highs. Except for the music they'd be as quiet as the tombs across the street. They'd try to enjoy themselves in the prison that they sort of knew was a prison, but whatever its drawbacks it was better than anything else they could imagine—and far better than hanging out in an old mansion on Emerson Street and watching their parents deepening their ennui with swizzle sticks for their double Manhattans.

They'd probably ODed long ago on stories about how Gramps started a jar company or built a better drill. The idea of having to go to some fine school and study every day was death. They preferred to hit themselves than to hit the books. I got all this schemed out, you see, without sending Dez on one of her spy missions.

Every now and then I think I should cry. I never do, because I keep my sense of humor as a sort of electric hair dryer against the tears. But I'm lonesome, and yet just about everybody I know who has "somebody" really has nobody. My parents are old enough that they're starting to question themselves about their vision for driving now. They had two boys and lots of hopes and expectations. Now they're losing courage even faster than they're losing their retinas. One lad, my older brother, died of AIDS— who knew? He never told me the how or why, but he invited my parents to think it was bad blood. As he told me in the hospital, with bated raspy breath, "I'm going to try to convince Mom and Pops that I've actually been Haitian all this time." The other lad, myself, dropped out of the college and became a fat cop, though at least I'm not hated around the shop. The problem is, Mom and Pops, however much they liked the idea of a college son, wouldn't have been proud of me if I'd become a professor of philosophy. A professor of *what*? Pops is the sort of guy who looks in the classifieds and tries to find out how many companies and shops out there are looking for philosophers. But they didn't relish me as a cop much either.

So it's all a pretty large spill, but when houses are a mess you can tear them down and start over or knock out some rooms or something. How do you do that with people? There used to be this huge junkyard in South Beloit. It was a real scene-stealer. You could see hundreds of abandoned cars piled up a mile away—the Red Sea of rust. OK, fine. But what do you do with junk people?

At headquarters we'd sometimes hear rumors that the Barbees and Mallows—the elder ones—would lament to others at the country club as to how their kids turned out this way, and we were told that their fellow Ricky Riches had told them not to fret: that kids were a crap shoot just like the games in Puerto Vallarta or it was just the culture—what do you expect when those permissive Democrats in Madison are in charge? They aren't in charge any more, so I'm not sure what the excuse du jour is now.

Well, that's as good a reason as any; the Democrats, I mean. Who knows what defective nails lurk within the wooden heart of man? We can just thank goodness that there's a Mallow tool for pulling them out, right? Last time I checked, they called it a hammer.

We wouldn't be talking to Jim and Julia again for a few days. They'd been charged and soon enough would see a judge and plead and try to get out on bail. If they wanted, they could come back and talk to Roger and me. We thought they might. We thought they might not. It sort of came down to whether Mr. Big had a real name or was just the Abominable Showman. We were betting on A.S. Well, I was. Roger said he thought there might have been a Mr. Big. Anyhow, we wouldn't know anything for several days. So before I know it, it's morning and time to talk to a real Mr. Big, in Rockford. His name was Andrew Drabble, and he may have been a world-class maker of box bottoms.

Or he may not have been. I thought not. Roger was sure he was. Roger seemed sort of sure of everything these days. But then he was a believer, mostly in Roger.

15: Drabbling On

Well, OK, so off we went at 9 AM to Rockford, there to call on the redoubtable Andrew Drabble, the great builder. He had his shop on the west side of Rockford, which might have disappointed Roger because he seemed keen on the trip, which I thought optional at best, and so I figured, at the time, that he wanted to go down State Street on the east side of town so he could see all the chain restaurant signs. You can't see enough Machine Shed and TGIF broadsides in life, right?

The west side of Rockford isn't an especially auspicious section of that community, third largest in Illinois; but the trip down has a few amenities, including a lot more scenery than you'll find off Interstate 90 and an occasional glimpse of the Rock River. Not that you actually see it, but you sort of know it's not far away. You could call it a semi-glimpse. The trip on State Highway 2 is grand on the other side of Rockford, where you get winding panoramic views of the mighty Rock on its way to the even mightier Mississippi at the Quad Cities. But we weren't going that far south.

And when we got to Drabble Construction Company headquarters it made Beloit Police Headquarters look magnificent. Our city hall building was not only three stories of red brick. It also had every floor receding a bit so that it looked as though it was a man in some small danger of falling over backwards and falling on some house that Abe Lincoln supposedly slept in. Drabble, in contrast, was a metal ranch house that looked like it had been glued to the ground by some sort of Super Elmer's. When we got to Mr. Drabble's office, however, after we had asked if he was in, we got a surprise.

Everything had been arranged in advance. We'd let Rockford cops know we were coming and that this was a routine inquiry. We'd left a message with Drabble himself, though he'd not replied. We were all set. When we were shown into his office we were amazed at its opulence. This was a small ranch house that looked like it had been been made of tin, though it was actually steel-enhanced aluminum. The office must have taken up over a third of the total space. The rest of it were a couple of clerks—this included the prim secretary whose hair bob looked as though it might be hurting her--and five cheap desktops.

But the office: carpeting so thick you could fall off the John Hancock building on it and not feel a thing; two or three obviously pricey Persian rugs (was one of them the source of Gloria's plump Persian cat?); a nearly wall-to-wall desk so that you wondered how he got behind it; some maybe rare and costly prints on the wall (French but for all I know, Albanian); and two Wisconsin elk sticking out of the tin and looking as though they were about as glad to be there as the Persian rugs or the file cabinets were. Andrew himself was no great beast. He was a small man with a mustache the bristles of which stood up like one of Colgate's best organic toothbrushes (are there such things?). He had Dracula teeth that he liked to show off, though when he did he seemed a rather obsequious vampire because he was a tiny guy. But he could snarl behind those dark gray eyes of his, which seemed as though it might have more coal than in all of Kentucky. His face was so miniature that at times it seemed like he was the Cheshire Cat slowly vaporizing off.

The guy's waist was so small he needed both his electric blue suspenders and an overweight black belt to hold his trousers up. The shirt was a fine white dress garment, but the pants were rumpled khakis, which seemed to be his only concession to the fact that he often had to visit dirty building sites.

All that, though, is what you observed before you heard him talk. This was not a guy unaccustomed to command. He was quite open with us, but it didn't seem to come from any sense that he was under duress and was afraid not to reveal stuff. Rather, it seemed to say, "I can speak frankly to you gentlemen because you are of no importance or danger to me. I'm the big shot here, not you. Don't be fooled, Roger Webb, by your six two strapping good looks. You're penniless compared to me. I run the orphanage and you're just a guest here if you're lucky."

"So we just, uh, wanted to let you know, if you didn't already, that your ex-wife, or wife rather, has been reporting these disturbances. It's all pretty vague at this point except for this one thing which we'll get to."

"And you want to know from me"—this was a rich basso when his size made you expect a clarinet—"if I know of anybody who would want to bother her."

"Uh, yes," I said, "that could be very helpful, yes." I noticed that Roger hadn't said a word, though he seemed to be enjoying the plush ochre armchair he'd taken.

"I know of nobody. Gloria is standoffish. She has few friends. She has no foes. I can't think of anyone. Of course I appreciate you taking the time to tell me this. What sort of disturbances?"

Now he was questioning us. The reversal had begun already.

"It's a bit fuzzy: a noise here, a rustling there, a shadow at the bedroom window."

"Which bedroom?"

Was this guy the chief of detectives?

"Uh, the nearest one to the west side."

"I think she's taken that one. She told me once. Please check. It would make sense that she'd hear something there if anywhere."

"Right. But you don't know of any enemies, right?"

"Right."

"Well, she found at that bedroom window—this was about two or three days ago—this box bottom." I produced it for the Vampire, Drabble, and the Silent Partner, Webb, who was studying the whole thing as though sizing up an enemy for himself.

"This looks like it might come from a box of—what do you call those mints that Marshall Fields used to make? Frango mints? But it could be a box of cookies. I suppose it could be a box of big staples. We use those here in the office. Our contracts are thick. Without the top it's a glossy white load of cardboard and that's about it. Where did you say she'd found this again?"

He was asking the questions.

"I said." I decided to push back. "I said it was by the west bedroom window."

"Inside or outside?"

Well, that would make a difference. "Outside."

"I'm glad it wasn't inside. That would be a bit sinister. How do you know she found it?"

"Come again?" Roger actually knew how to speak

"How do you know she found it?"

"Well"—me again, though I noticed Roger agitating a little next to me—"she told us about it."

"She told you she found it."

"Yes."

"Well, that settles it. She found it. Does she think this, uh, disturber left it there?"

"She thinks so."

"So it would be someone who likes mints or cookies or staples. That should give you gentlemen some real leads. Look, men. Gloria and I have been estranged for over six months. If you ask her, she'll tell you that I found her to be much too predictable and housewifey. It's true that she's a corn-fed girl of the Plains, still quite attractive. The truth is, I've never found her boring a day in her life. She's going through a thing that lots of us go through. What's the point of it all? Is this all there is? She had gotten to feeling down; it was sort of depression mixed with what her doctor called free-floating anxiety. I thought she needed space. I think above all she needs to ask herself if marriage to me is going to be the only real achievement of her life. Or does she want to do other things? She's talked of viola lessons. With me around she wouldn't be able to work this out. So I've given her time alone to think. I think we'll be back together by early winter, though it may cost me an expensive viola. But I think the college up there can find someone to give her lessons if I'm willing to pay enough, and I will. She says I find her boring. That's her sadness talking. I don't."

"But how do you, er, explain this box bottom?"

"Well, first, as a man who has to observe materials carefully in order to use them to build tract houses and offices, I'll say that it is a bottom. If it were a top, it would likely have a label on it. But you mean how do I explain how she came to find it? No idea. I can't. Someone left it there. I don't know who."

"Are you saying she didn't find it?" Roger again. Why was he being a tad aggressive with this little count?

"If she said she found it, Sergeant, she found it. She's depressed. She's not crazy. I predict," he added with pearl incisors, "that she'll become the best viola player in Rock County, Wisconsin."

16: Darkness Beckons

"What a prick," said Roger back in the car.

I couldn't precisely disagree, but I thought it was time I used some of my college lad knowledge on my seething partner.

"That was my impression, too, Sergeant. But I think this trip was justified. He's an estranged husband. His wife has reported things. He's got money and influence. We were right to let him know what was coming down, although not much has come down and nothing is coming down right now."

Roger scrunched up his eye-catching face. He almost looked ugly with a scowl like that. He was my passenger, and by now we were headed through a short tunnel of trees back north to headquarters. The tunnel soon passed, and we were in the open again. The land next to the road was so flat that you would almost think you could have driven just as well on either one. It was getting near noon. It had cooled. It gets like that in August sometimes. Fall starts early this far north, but sometimes it lasts until December One, when you get a blizzard. It's simply marvelous when you get the new snow and the old leaves slung into your face at once.

The air hadn't put Roger's temper on ice. He was demanding to know what I meant by the irreverent statement that nothing had really come down. He felt disrespected. But hey, logic has to make its debut somehow. So I continued.

"Mrs. Drabble hasn't really seen anybody for sure. She found the bottom of a box. We don't know that she did find it. She says she found it by this sinister window. We don't know that. We have no idea where this thing came from or what it's the bottom to, or what it means. We got nothing. Look, Roger, I'm not trying to lay the 'hysterical woman' act on you here. I'm just saying we've really got very few facts. We're chasing our tails, and quite possibly we are pursuing our hind ends for no good reason at all. In fact, old friend, chasing one's tail is generally not a particularly reasonable activity."

"I've got a bad feeling about this. Let's remember that that's a butt hole back there in that trailer ranch house of his, with the elks reduced to ash trays."

I thought this was pretty poetic for Roger, even if I didn't get the ashtray part. But zeal can make one eloquent. I felt slightly encouraged, too: Roger called Drabble a butt hole and I was talking about chasing hind ends and the box had a bottom. I was beginning to see a pattern here.

"He said the bottom could have come from a box of Frango mints, cookies, or even staples Well, Jeremy old pal, they don't put cookies in boxes this small, and they don't put big staples in boxes this glossy. That leaves mints, except that he said mints because he knew they were those Godiva chocolates. He said Marshall Fields to put us off the scent."

"Actually, I think Fields has been closed for years."

"There you go, Sergeant Dropsky. This shows the guy is even more misleading."

"Or maybe he misremembered about Fields. Or maybe they still make those mints under Target or whoever owns Fields now.

Face it, Roger: what Andrew Drabble said about this box bottom means nothing at all. You have a bad feeling. I've got some good logic. There may be something here. You may be right. But if there's something here it hasn't shown its little elk's head yet, OK? We haven't found the smoking gun, or even the smoking ash tray."

"That's because that little elk's head is in the dark. You can't see it, Jeremy. But it's there. I can sense it."

"How? Can you smell it or hear it? What do little elks' heads smell like?"

"I can sense it."

He looked over at me as though I'd gassed the Kurds and then he said, "Sometimes I think we weren't meant to be partners. You're maybe my best friend because I can tell you anything, unlike my brother who I couldn't tell anything to. But we're not meant to be partners in a police unit."

"Why not?"

I swear this was rehearsed: "Because you've got a big gut but won't ever follow it."

I nearly swerved off the road. If the Rock River had been near enough we'd have gone swimming.

Roger was laughing, too, without joy.

And with that we fell into silence for the rest of the journey. You might want to call it a dark silence. Be my guest.

Back at the station trivia reigned. A guy had run over a cat near the Eclipse Center (our combination shopping mall, public library, and conference center) and had a guilty conscience and wanted to confess. They told him he had not committed a crime, and they were right. But if it had been Dez, he would have committed a crime, and I'd have had to find a way to run him in. That was *my* dark thought of the day.

One of the assistant deans at Beloit College was there to report that outsiders were getting onto campus and putting "Beloit College Sucks" on the restroom walls and wanted to know if we had any advice about how to stop it. The college has its own security system, and we tend to defer to them. I don't know how or why this dean turned to us. We recommended white paint, or turquoise if the walls happened to be turquoise, or even if they weren't turquoise.

It was like that the rest of the day. Beloit has a mini-urban quality. We're racially diverse, like Chicago or Milwaukee; and some of our bars get a little frisky late at night, also similar to the great metros to our east. But we're no big city. So don't expect the glamour of nine murders a day. We're not Chicago's South Side. Not even Milwaukee's North one.

Late August, and the nights start to draw in noticeably early. So by half past seven it was good and dark. As I was feeding myself, and Dez, and dreaming of Mary and wondering what sorts of chocolates Gloria Drabble was feeding her cat, I wondered what this premature darkness meant. Was there an elk's head descending on River City, and was it Andrew Drabble's elk's head? Or was there some sort of giant Frango mint shrouding the city of Beloit, Wisconsin? Was Roger taking an extra hour or two at the bar, showing off for Joe and dissing and frustrating Mary with the short brown hair even more?

Damned! I wished I'd known about the Drabbles when they were still together. I could have sent Dez out to far east Shopiere Road to look in on them and report back to me. What was their life really like? Was it what Mr. Drabble—little Big Man—said it was? Did Gloria say to him that he was bored with her because she was Ms. Redbook or Ladies' Home Journal and he wanted kink? Did he say to her, "No, you just want more out of life than marriage to me. You want viola lessons. I still love you.." Is that what he said to her? None of this made the remotest sense to me.

But it didn't seem to be anything criminally wrong. Gloria and Andrew were not cooking lithium cough syrup the way Julie and Jimmy Rich were. Still, we can file all of this, all of it, under "Lifestyles of the Rich But Not So Famous in Beloit, Wisconsin."

But let's think about it for a minute, OK? She says, "You want somebody you can tie up and anally penetrate," and he says, "No, you just want to become Beloit's answer to Yo-Yo Ma (does he or she play the viola or the cello or neither?)." It's like either two totally different conversations or it's like one of those, what do you call them, "absurdist" plays where nobody makes any sense and that's what makes it "art."

Andrew and Gloria weren't crooks. But one or both of them seemed to be feeding us a line, and I wasn't finding it nourishing while Roger wanted to go back for seconds.

Dez could have come back and told me the truth. But now Andrew and Gloria are separated, and there's nothing for Dez to see of the two of them together. And I've got to admit that asking her to go all the way out there would have been pretty damned thoughtless of me. I don't want to take my brilliant orange tabby for granted. She's what I've got.

But she does go all over the city at night. After dinner she heads out the cat door and doesn't come back sometimes until the wee hours when she jumps on my back for some dry snack food, which, by the way, I always keep on the bed, along with some Korn Kurls for me, too. We've had regular feasts at 3:27:16 AM., Dezzie and I.

And when tonight Dez goes out she will do so in darkness, as though—I don't know—she's exploring the black laboratory of Roger Webb's suspicions. What is Roger suspicious of? For starters, he's suspicious of Mary, who wants him to be a human being instead of a cop. For another, he's suspicious of Mr. Drabble. He's suspicious of life. He thinks it's served him up a dish of scorpions or something, and he's maybe waiting for someone or something to snatch the platter of scorpions away and replace it with obese shrimp and green ketchup. Let's see. I'm getting well onto thirty, but Roger is at least five years older. He's due for a mid-life crisis. It's on schedule, like the 9:55 Van Galder bus to O'Hare that leaves from the McDonald's in South Beloit and takes you, in just ninety minutes, to a place where you'll see turbans and burkas and pinstriped suits and all the other stuff you'll never catch hiding out here in River Town.

As Dez padded about the city of Beloit she probably realized she'd become infected, just as I had, by Roger's descent into the night. The ducks on the Rock River and on Turtle Creek swam in black flowing waters. The tears left on the counters of the bars—of liquid giggles or desperation—had turned into liquid tar. As Beloit College was starting up, some overseas freshman far from home sat on an Indian Mound and looked into the dusk and wondered which direction her old bedroom in Rawanda or Hong Kong is in. The Eclipse Center was closed for the day and stirred with memories of a once thriving Beloit Mall, including the shadowy ones of a Radio Shack where once two young men had been gunned dead because the trigger man had wanted a police scanner and didn't want to pay for it. There was even a Mr. Steak in that mall once—dark sirloins culled from cows gone efficiently into oblivion. In Oakwood Cemetery and other Beloit graveyards the ghosts peeked out to see how night it had become. They could chat with one another at last. No one would disturb the first president of Beloit College or the Greek professor who had once been found dead and nude in his office and maybe murdered, or the brother of the great painter Norman Rockwell, who's also racked out there, or so I'm told. What did they have to say to one another in that night long shade? "Are you starting to find me to be a bore? Did you ever get to take those viola lessons? Someone left a box of Frango mints for me the other night, but I can't eat them because then they'll know I'm a ghost but still alive." Is that what all the corpses say to each other in Beloit, Wisconsin?

Only Dez know for sure. Only she knows what really goes on in the smoky murk of Beloit on a late summer's night.

Actually, though, she hasn't gone out at all. She's sleeping on my soft and beefy lap. I don't think Roger's twilight has gotten to her. I think it's gotten to me.

Roger said he was roiled with bad feelings. Now I have them, too.

17: Chamomile Cocktail

Life went on at the big police station near the Illinois border, or maybe I should say life didn't go on, since inebriated fist fights on the near west side and complaints about heavy metal noise from next door (two of these in one week, from different neighbors) hardly count as life in any meaningful sense. Oh, there was also news that a guy whose DNA matched a 2003 crime was finally on his way back, cuffed, to Rock County; but that was really an old, exhausted story by now. Those are the kinds of things we had for a while. When I say "life in any meaningful sense" that's my old college boy talking. Do you think I'm getting bored with my job? Well, I am. But I somehow see myself better suited to weighing meth crystals for the evidence boys and girls, and even having sane feelings about chocolate candy and viola lessons, than to sitting in a classroom in the World Affairs Center or Morse-Ingersoll Hall and offering a disquisition on what Wittgenstein meant by "The world is everything that is the case."

But then good things come to those who wait—bad things, too. And so while life "in the meaningful sense" was not happening down at the station, it suddenly cropped up in my own shabby living room. I was settling down one evening at about 2000 hours (that's 8:00 for you amateurs) when none other than Roger himself knocked on my fiberglass pseudo-wooden door. Now this might not seem like much to you, especially since you know I see Roger all day. But he'd rarely stopped in. I never had him and Mary over for dinner because I don't cook, and she's allergic to cat dander, bless her darling little heart. They'd had me over because they felt sorry for me. This was only the third or fourth time that Roger had even seen the inside of my little place. He saw I was surprised, but he got right to it. "Mind if I sit down in one of your luxurious arm chairs?" Luxurious they were not. They were straight-up chairs with not a lot of cushion and some shaky arms, though one of them had wheels on it for mobility in case you didn't want to get on your feet in order to see the radio better. Oh, and there was a rocker: my pride and joy from St. Vincent's. Roger took the rocker. Roger the Rocker: what beat did he have to offer?

"Hey, dude. I don't know why you're here. Can't be good. You want to tell me something? You're bored with Mary again? If so, can I spend some time with her? I like to be bored. [Note: This was the first time I'd ever said anything like this to anyone other than Dez, and I shouldn't have said it to Roger.] Do you want something to drink? I've got vodka. I've got chamomile tea. You can have either or both. How about a Vodka Chamomile? I hear they're just the thing now down on Rush Street in the East Loop."

To my surprise he said yes. It was clear Roger was going to surprise me this evening. It seemed his mission in life. I only had the vodka, and I only had the tea. Other than that, it was water. I was all out of the most fattening Orange Crush I could find. How could I have let that happen?

He sniffed the steaming witches' brew of herbs and Mr. Boston. "I stopped by to say that Mary and I are through."

"You're a moron."

"Yeah, well, you would say that, Jeremy. That's because you're immature. Look, you and I have always been straight with each other. That's the best thing about our teamwork. You tell me I go by the gut too much, and I'm telling you now that you're immature—I mean, about what we should call affairs of the heart."

"OK. I'm immature and logical. You're an instinctual moron. Go on."

"Ha, ha, ha." He wasn't laughing. "You see, Jer, in your vast inexperience you look at Mary and you see cute and jolly and sexy"—he didn't say that her short hair might have also brought out my latent homosexuality—"and you think how could anyone not love *this*. But that's because you're thinking with your penis in a way; that, plus you've never been married or dated much. There's more to a marriage than just the looks and even the sex and the good humor, sir."

"There is? I'd take either or both. I have neither. Maybe your problem is that you lack experience in lonely bachelorhood. Ever think of it that way, Roger?"

"I have been a bachelor. I've been married. I have more experience than you do."

"Go on. You just here to give me a news bulletin or do I also get the expert commentary?"

"You get both. I'm here to tell you because I like you loads. I respect you. I'm here to explain myself, too; or hear myself explain myself."

Roger snarled when he said this. It ruined his early Warren Beatty face. I wondered if Thomas Jefferson snarled when he said he was going to give mankind a decent account of why the colonies were divorcing Britain. There goes the college boy again.

"OK. Go on, moron."

"OK. I will. Look, Mary doesn't do it for me. Now you'll think I'm selfish, going on about me. But she doesn't know who I am, or who I want to be. I want to be the best cop around these here parts. She wants me to be something out of Dr. Phil. In leaving her I'm making sure I can focus on my priorities, OK? I'm doing people a favor. If I'm a good cop I'm doing people a favor."

"You're a workaholic. You're in love with your job. You're proud of your gut. She doesn't appreciate that. She wants a human being. Is that it?"

"Maybe. She wants me to be what my Aunt Helen wanted me to be. Did I ever tell you that she more or less raised me in Milwaukee after my parents divorced? I lived with my mom, but Aunt Helen was really the parent. I probably stayed with her over half the time. She always said the main thing was to be a good person. At first I liked that. But as I grew up and got some ambitions to make a difference in this world, I started to resent her. Her 'be a good person' was one big Sunday School stifle, I can tell you that."

"OK, so now you've married Aunt Helen, is that it? And I'll bet Aunt Helen was really pious—your mom's sister, right—and you think Mary is really pious, and you've got the two confused. Well, Mary isn't really pious. She's just got needs, imbecile."

I liked Roger because you could talk to him this way, and he'd take it but come back at you.

"Well, I think, Jer, it comes down to values. I value being a great cop. I've got a mission here. You see the job as something *you* do because you can't imagine yourself a schoolboy. It fell into your lap. You get to wear a badge and be a smart-ass. That suits you, OK? Not me. I see this job as a calling, man, as a way to save people. You see Beloit as the same old same old: the domestic fights, the bar fights, the shootings—just more pooped-out crapola in River City. I don't. I see being a cop as community service. I want to be great at it. I want to solve big cases. I want to run down really bad guys. I want to keep people from being injured by really bad guys. Someday I want to be the best cop in Milwaukee and known for that. I just need the one big break. I don't want to die getting a Hubby of the Year award in Beloit, Wisconsin."

"You've got ambitions. You want to be a hero. Did you ever think that a cop that wants to be a hero is a menace to public safety?" I still can't believe I said that, and now I wish I had repeated it.

"Yeah, you could say that. But this is me, Jeremy. You see policing as one damn thing after another. I see policing as a story, of a man's rise; of a single man's coming onto the scene to save the day. Mary doesn't get that, and she wants to turn me into a goddamned sissy."

Roger Webb had never ever saved the day, though he did save me once at crazy Bobby Boso's house and never got any credit because it wasn't something he did—it was something I *didn't* do. He was a copper just like me. He wanted to be Mighty Mouse Cop. It still amazes me that *he* didn't want to barge into the Boso place, and you know: I think he would have if he'd really thought Bobby was still gunning for somebody. Now that I look back on it, I see that caution was easy for Roger that night because he didn't really think there was anything to be reckless about. He's a tricky fellow, Roger is.

But yeah, by now he'd done too many domestics and burglaries for too long; faced too many unsolvable cases; was having his mid-life existential crisis (my college boy act again); and had gone all romantic hero on me—and on Mary, too, and she wasn't having it. Now he really was on the cover of those romantic bodice-rippers that Dez told me Rose read.

Roger decided that Roger had to be Roger. In time the fever would break, but in the meantime he was going to break his marriage. Once Roger's high temperate had turned to sweat, he'd be OK in a way. (Well, that's what I thought at the time.) But the problem was this: Mary was something that all the king's horses and men wouldn't be able to do a frigging thing about.

She wanted a husband, not a hero.

Roger might have become a low-level drunk. I mean, who else accepts a mix of chamomile and vodka? I even think that Roger was a little insane at this point. And I think he knew it, too. He had to do something big in order to regain control of himself. I mean, this guy, my beloved partner, the Brad Cruise of the force, had to do something big; something crazy; something really splitting, in order to find the reset button. All this talk about saving somebody like they do on TV cop shows—this was loony-tunes.

But hey, I thought at the time, sometimes you've got to let the crazy out, right, in order to find Sane Ave again.

This was also as lunatic as chamomile vodka, which Roger was obligingly sipping. Hell, he even seemed to enjoy the stuff.

"Why don't you bother to save *Mary* if you want to be a hero?"

"She doesn't want me to save her. She wants me, like, to go on Oprah with her and confess my feelings. She reads too many women's magazines."

"And you've seen too many cop shows."

"Sometimes, Jeremy, we all have to ride our own high country."

Was that from a cigarette ad? And the only high country around here is Big Hill Park, and horses aren't allowed there except maybe on Saturdays.

Roger wanted to do something big. In time, I was sure, he would come to his senses and get small again. His second wife would beat the nuttiness out of him and tell him never to sin again in thinking of himself as Mr. Hero, *or* she'd be mousy and tell him that he was saving humanity while investigating a break-in on Liberty Avenue that he'll never solve.

We traded a few more jabs, and he left, telling me out the door that his decision was irrevocable and that he'll be looking for a room to rent. I was glad he didn't want to stay with me. He wouldn't know how to handle Dez's nightly reports, and my one spare bed was a couch that resembled mashed potatoes, color and all, with too many lumps in the serving..

18: *Crystal Chandeliers*

Friday night in Beloit, late August, might have been dark, at least as Dez and I saw it. But the sun came up on Saturday morning, as it often does, big and bright, like a dog ready to play and wagging sure that everything, just everything, is going to be swell. My weekends are spent in solitude: a Denise Mina crime novel; whatever sports are on out of Madison, Milwaukee, or Chicago; occasionally a trip next door to old Mrs. Windcomb's house for soup and crackers and scrambled eggs. Good for me: not fattening at all. She lost two boys in Nam, and so you can't not go and hear her talk about them. I'm sort of her beau, and it's a nasty job to have *me* as a beau but someone should sign up. She's so old, poor baby, you could put nickels in her wrinkles and never find them again. Sometimes on weekends I get guilty about dropping out of college and go back over Wittgenstein's distinction between reason and cause, hoping this time I'll understand it. I never do. The great thinker's reasoning is as beyond me as trying to figure out why Roger doesn't love Mary any more. I never fail to skip church, which used to be up near the college, but that one closed and has merged with one on the near west side. The old mainstream Protestant churches are dying, along (they say) with the sensible middle class, whatever that means. I read stuff but then forget what I never grasped in the first place. I just can't recall, with any detail, all the stuff "they" have told me, but I still pay attention to them just in case *they* may know something I don't.

I'm much more of an expert on meth than on the sensible middle class. In fact, the rise of meth might also be traced to the decline of the sensible middle class and the mainline Protestant churches. But that's not the side of meth I know. And on Monday morning, when the divorcing Roger and I checked into work in order, first and always, to hear Rose tell for the ten thousandth time of how she'd like to push Susan's chariot into the surging Rock from one of the bluffs in Big Hill Park, meth was the number one subject.

Julia and Jimbo had been arraigned, and they'd gotten bail. They'd found a catapult at the Rock County jail and had ridden out on it. For them, at least for now, no more resort time in Janesville at the corner of Routes 14 and 51. I wonder how a couple of upper class pseudo-swells felt about having to listen to the rowdy wails and ever profane chitchat of creeps from other corridors of life's big mall. Of course bail was steep, but their parents had the green so that was that. But their lawyers had thrown in something else, and we were arguing about why they had. The attorneys told the judge that JJ just might, might, be able to supply some dirt on Mr. Big. They didn't say it like that of course. They used some fuzzy legalese. Why did they do it in the first place?

I said it was because the lawyers weren't sure the wealth and influence of the parents would be enough. These two were always into some kind of filth, but so far everything had been reduced to misdemeanors—even the grass sales were so diminished as long as our fun couple agreed not to do it again. That's the power of jelly jars and machine drills that once made a mint. This was different. This was cooking meth, with burgeoning proof that they had sold it. Already, neighbors were giving us chapter and verse about all the cat's asses that had come to and gone from that dump.

So I figured the lawyers put in the stuff about turning state's evidence on higher ups in order to sweeten a deal they weren't sure they could get otherwise. They likely didn't need to do this. Julia and James had been caught with crystals in kitty litter containers, but their parents had crystal chandeliers, and the latter trumped the former. And all this I proclaimed, round and about the station. Hear ye, hear ye!

Roger disagreed. He said he was pretty sure there was a Mr. Big. He told me no self-respecting Janesville lawyer would possibly offer a suggestion like that unless there *was* something. I thought Rog was on meth himself. He'd lost his judgment. They could always make a vague proffer and say their clients had changed their minds. I thought Roger out of his mind with his opinion about this, but later, in view of what came down, I realized he was crazy like a fox. He knew what he was doing.

But the truth was, there could have *been* a Mr. Big. I didn't think so, and Charlie Baxter didn't think so, and the Feds we talked to didn't think so either. Yet on Roger's side of the argument there had been two other meth shacks in Beloit and South Beloit of late. I saw this as free enterprise doing its lovely work. Meth gives rushes to people who think short-term. My God: we're back to the sensible middle class, aren't we—the closing of the local Presbyterian Church or something. I mean, the sensible middle class thinks *long* term. The sensible middle class knows a rush for the next five minutes means they've just paid a bundle for something they could be using to buy car insurance or put Junior through college. The sensible middle class (from now on, s.m.c.) just doesn't go in for five-minute feel goods. The s.m.c.'s admiration of that sort of thing is under control. But I'm told they're dying off. That's what *they* tell me.

But your wayward youth; your small-time crooks who get ahead with a lucky break-in; your guys and gals who want to have sex for five days in a row—these not so solid citizens go in for the Big Rush. I've never tried it—though I sometimes think I should because it's a sure cure for obesity—but I've been told that nothing you'll ever feel will ever feel better than this for a wee time. If you shoot yourself up or smoke it, it's right now. If you snort it or pill it, you'll need to wait a little bit and it won't be as high octane, though it'll stay with you a little longer. Whatever your trouble: farts, guilt, the common cold, failure, lovesickness, impotence—meth whisks all of it away. Actually, it's not a bad deal if you can just be satisfied with a momentary reprieve. But few are. They want it again and again. Once you get free of pain for five minutes—and that's what we really crave in this country—then you want the same nirvana for five days or five years.

As a cop I've got to say that none of this bothers me a bit, except for the unfortunate fact that people kill other people for this stuff, or they kill other people if they don't deliver or pay for this stuff; or they get downright scary when they're off this stuff, or they get awfully reckless and frightening when they're *on* this stuff, too. It's a menace to public safety. And of course it's against the law. Did I forget to say that? I can't imagine why.

I'm sure all the liberals and other advanced thinkers at places like Beloit College think we should just legalize this stuff. That will give meth contracts government protection. You can sue instead of having to shoot. And the government can collect tax dollars from the sales. That just sounds lovely, sort of like Roger's notion of how much better life might be if he didn't have Mary ragging on him to be the next Phil Donahue or something. But legalizing won't solve much. The stuff is just too strong. It makes idiots out of everyone who snorts or shoots it. They got to have more. And more and more and more. The sensible middle class Protestants are right about the perils of meth. Too bad their church closed. It's a massive rambling sandstone structure that once jutted its vast domain, in heady confidence, around the corner block, erected to say that on this rock a church shall be built against which the gates of Hell will never stand. The exterior is dull as though to say, "Look for no rushes here—only the gloom of virtue." Now I've heard it's a meeting center, but at least they don't cook crack on the giant kitchen stove in the back. I remember that stove. I used to go back there before services. It was hot. It scared me. I thought this must be what Hell looked like. I thought the gates of Hell were *in* the church, no matter what the Bible said to the contrary.

Well, I'm rambling, like the church's preachers once did, but the demand for this super dew is so great, and the capacity to supply it is so relatively simple, that you don't need a Mr. Big At Large in order to have sinister cookeries pop up everywhere. So I think Julia and Jimmy were just freaky little capitalists. They didn't need the money. They just wanted the ride. But they were also good Americans: they went into business for themselves. They didn't know shit about any Mr. Big.

Roger was the only one who thought otherwise. But Roger was living even sunny days as if they were midnight these days. He could have used a snort himself. Me, I'd have settled for just one dehydrated kiss from Mary. Some lucky bastards don't know they're lucky bastards.

But then just maybe I had misunderstood Roger, the lucky bastard.

19: Mint Condition

Our police station isn't remarkable. It's got the usual facilities you'd find in almost any of them, at least in the US of A: the lockers, the locked doors where they keep extra ammo, the interrogation rooms, the holding cells for when somebody a little frisky comes in or is hauled in, computers and clerks for record-keeping, and offices for the chief of detectives and for the chief of police and his assistant (magnificent cubicles for Roger and me, alas). You go in there on a Sunday afternoon when not much hops, and you'll think it's almost any corporate or government office. Even when it buzzes a bit, it doesn't take on much that any Hollywood producer would want to film. Early this week they brought in a guy who'd solicited sex from a kid. He was a tall husky guy with a mustache that looked like the shrubbery you can never quite cut back, and a lope that got frustrated by the leg chains. Everyone, including Rose, looked up briefly, and there might have been a barely discernible shaking of heads. But mostly people just went back to what they were doing. The presence of evil just didn't seem to make a dent in the official consciousness of a small city cop shop. What would evil be doing here? Why would it bother to come to the banks of the Rock River when it has things to do in the Middle East? As for Rose, I'm sure she thought this guy was bad but that Susan was much worse.

This guy had only harmed fifteen year-old girls. Susan had harmed Rose.

But on this day—only a few days after we'd had our chat with Andrew Drabble, the Little Giant—Roger and I had another date with Julie and Jim. They'd gotten out on bail. They didn't have to talk to us. We had to get their permission and that of their lawyers. We didn't think we'd get it. We were a little surprised when they all said yes. Our invite was routine anyhow.

To me, this proved that they had no added info, despite what Roger thought. Why did they come in for a chat? I think it was because their lawyers had told them to make as nice as possible with us; that we had the goods on them and their only chance was to come off as sweet boy and girl. I could hardly wait to see how they were dolled up for trial. I'm thinking something out of a Nordstrom catalogue—better make that Penney's, as a local juror will think Nordstrom's too stuck up. As for dope on a higher-up in the meth trade, forget about it. These two got nothing to trade Blind Justice other than their high-priced lawyers and scrubbed-up good looks. They'll promise never to cook anything again, not even toast, and say they'll never even think about putting crystals in a disused plastic litter box. And they'll each get five years and be out in 1.5.

Most of the poor slobs they were selling to will spend most of their lives in and out of jail. Justice is blind indeed.

They came in promptly at 10, and their lawyers from J-ville said right away, of course, that this was a courtesy call and that their clients wouldn't be saying much other than good morning, if that.

And so I decided to do some talking of my own. "Went by your cook shack again the other day, kids. I got to say that you really know how to pick 'em. That place has been damp for years. Does it even have a foundation? It seemed kneeling in surrender to the good earth. The crack down the front is a work of art, and you'd have to go to an art museum to find a modern sculpture like that drainpipe snorkeling down the side. You'd think that with your parents' bread you could have set up a mansion for your sales, with maybe a neon sign out front: GET YOUR LIFE METHED UP HERE!"

One of the lawyers grimaced and grinned. He and I had exchanged several of these knowing looks. These looks said, "You and I, Fat Jeremy, both know this is all useless, but we're getting paid, I more than you, to go through it." Meanwhile, the D.A. wanted us to ask, again, about Mr. Big. He didn't think there was any such person, but the two of them had brought it up so rules and regulations insisted that the local prosecutors had to follow it up. We could have made JJ come in and talk to us, of course, but we decided to play nice in order to vamp for time. So we sent them an engraved invitation so that they could decline and we could stall before we had to report back to the county attorney's office again.

I love bureaucracy. Reminds me of my life. Mostly pointless but with a lot of persistence.

This procedural dance between the forces of truth, justice and the American way and the forces of evil is especially apt when the two perps come from old vinegar bottle and jackhammer money.

"So," I went on, "I assume you two weren't doing this on your own, is that right? Did your parents bankroll you? Should they go behind the bars of the slammer, too? We could always make them gold-plated, you know, just for them."

Jimmy had put on a little weight. Getting his demeanor sanitized and chocking himself full of some Emerson Street top ground had given him a new improved giant economy size look. His face was fuller. He'd had a haircut. He'd found some professorial wire rims to make him look mild-mannered. He spoke.

"Our lawyers here have told us to say little. Julia and I will have to know more about what the D.A. has in mind for us before we can say much else. What protections can you afford us? That sort of thing is what I mean." He said this with his very best nice-boy imitation. And his very best wasn't very good.

"Oh," said Roger, "you mean witness protection programs, is that it? Well, kids, I hope you're serious. I want to be serious, too. There are such programs. I can't go into any detail, you understand. But you don't have to give up your lives if you want to save the public from the big bad guys who bankroll this sort of pixie dust."

My God! Roger sounded like he was from the F.B.I. or something. His inner Scoutmaster had finally come out. He actually believed this crapola about higher-ups, masterminds in pouchy deep purple double-breasted suits with black and sinister ties, pulling the strings on hundreds of drug houses in northern Illinois and southern Wisconsin. And he seemed sure that the little rich fry, Julia and James, had actually been in the presence of these potent plug-uglies, making oral deals with them to become the greatest meth chefs since Colonel Sanders had retired from fried chicken. Or was this a version of Roger's hero act?

Roger had good reason—well, reason anyhow (I don't know about good) for pushing this line. I didn't know it at the time.

I still don't quite know where J&J got the idea to open a meth kitchen. But it didn't come from any mastermind in Rockford or Milwaukee. It came because they couldn't think of anything else trifling and anti-social to do. It came because this was yet another way to frig over their parents—was it to avenge themselves on rich bitches that liked Riviera Maya better than they liked their own rotten kids and who can blame them?

Julia and Jim smiled, as did their lawyers, on cue. It seemed as though they'd practiced. One of the lawyers must have said, "At some point one of these fuzzes might take your offer of further info seriously. If one of them says anything about that, make sure you're courteous about it."

But of course the smile was totally non-committal, so I jumped in as the Chris Farley bad cop as opposed to the Jon Hamm good one. "As for protection, guys, I'm sure the Wisconsin prison system will do its best to guard you. Do we have anything else to do here today?"

Nobody said anything, so the conference was over in five minutes.

I was in a lousy mood—bad cold. I just hate them in early September when it's still hot enough to make your stuffiness even woolier, and not yet cold enough for everybody else to get sick and give you some sneezy company. So added to my bulk was a wheezy nose and lungs that felt like a little coal dust had maybe decided to become a guest.

I told Roger I was going home to take a nap. He said we had an appointment with Coach Ellis Duvall at 1 about a fairly routine hit-and run. I told him to change it to 2. He grimaced and agreed.

I don't like to take cold meds. They make me drowsy, an occupational hazard for a member of the peace officers community. I was fading anyhow. A great pulmonary plague had decided to occupy my big town, the one with the cheap Sears suitcoat draped around it. I needed rest, a cup of instant, and I'd be ready to let Roger wheel me to our next appointment. It was his turn to drive.

I got home, gave Dez a half tin of California Festival wet, slept, perchance to dream. Dez curled at bed's end. I told her to stop nibbling my toes. A big viral boy needs the paradise that only a lonely soft Beloit mattress can supply.

I slept several fathoms under for over an hour and soon, perchance, began to dream. *Paul and Gladys Wartenburg were at it again over on Central. Gladys wound her arms and fists up like a merry-go-round on speed (or maybe some of the JJ's meth) and tried to land a punch. Fred yelped for help. Susan appeared and, taking sides, tried to run down Gladys with her wheelchair. (How she got it up the steps to the porch I don't know, but you do know how dreams come down.) Rose came from nowhere and told Susan to mind her own business, whereupon Susan ran over Rose who, fatter than I am even, fell backwards squealing over Fred, who must have felt that he'd be better off pummeled by his irate wife of over fifty years. None other than Andrew Drabble appeared in his tiny grandeur and admonished Rose; told her to lay off the Frangos and suggested to all of them—both squabbling couples—that they'd all find peace in viola lessons.* All of this slapstick seemed reasonable to me. In my slumber I accepted it all as the law of nature. *Of course* this would happen, and in just this way. It was only much later that I mused upon the absence of Roger and Mary and Gloria from this dream, but then Charlie Baxter hadn't been in it either, so so what? Later, I thought Roger being missing was some sort of bad sign. An omen, even.

I woke smiling at the ingenuity of this fantasy. It was *my dream* after all. I felt wonderful. Only when Dez pounced on my chest did I get reminded of the cold, which weighed a ton. But by the time I'd had a quick cup of java and gotten into my near-powerless Nissan I realized that I was good to go until at least mid-afternoon. I parked and met Roger, per previous deal, in the lot.

For was it not so that Roger and I did have a call to make, no later than 2 P.M? It was out Turtle Creek way, towards the Golden Ghetto east of Beloit; the solid state of 60s ranches and 90s McMansions. This was the center of Beloit's professional class. Nobody obscenely rich lived out here for the most part. The super-wealthy, such as they were, had places in Florida or Arizona or lived on far east Emerson as did JJ's folks. That was one hundred percent prehistoric money.

A kid from out this creek area had done a hit-and-run. The child, a five year old, was OK; was going to live with no permanently ill effects. The driver was sixteen. He couldn't decide whether to drive off guilty fast or guilty slow, so he did something in between. His license plate was noted. He too was out on bail, but the D.A. needed background for sentencing. His next-door neighbor was the retired high school football coach. He had known this kid for years. What could he tell us about him? Would he be a repeat offender? The Rock County Attorney said he was dying to know. For all I cared, as a cop wearing some influenza along with his badge, he could keep on dying. But this was part of the job that, when I dropped out of Beloit College, I was dying to do.

Death is relative.

You couldn't have found a more generic ranch house than this one. It was the sort of turd brown wooden job that had decided it just couldn't get any flatter, as though it was trying to be a home and be Kansas all in one. You wanted to put it on its side so that it would at least have some height somewhere. There weren't even any steps to get up to the front door. Everything, you might say, was on the level. Maybe it was supposed to reflect the personality of the old coach, who'd retired a few years back. He too was supposed to be on the level.

Coach Ellis Duvall was at home by himself. He greeted us with hugs. He knew everybody in town and assumed all Beloiters were fans of the Purple Knights. "Sue isn't here," he said, "but let me make you some Folger's." It wasn't Folger's, but the coach must have thought all coffee was, somehow. His crew cut was gray by now. He had on what could only be called big glasses, black horn rims that surely could have been a match for a big heart, though it was said to be golden, not black. He smiled, mostly teeth and a prissy little mouth.

"You're here to talk about Jimmy Grayson, next door. Great kid. Wish I could have coached him. Made a mistake. I'll try to help you guys out."

Roger and I eyed each other for a nanosecond. We hadn't agreed on much of late, especially concerning whether or not the Rich Kids could give us the Mr. Meth; but on this we concurred. The Coach wasn't to help *us*. He was to help little Jimmy Grayson if he could. I sort of wondered if the D.A. would let himself be bent by the long beloved Purple Knights coach. I thought not, as he was now the ex-coach. What have you done for me this morning?

Roger said we'd have to eschew the Folger's. We had limited time. We were just there to gather—let's be blunt—a quasi-exonerating statement about a kid who'd plowed into a small boy and tried to get away with it. Yeah, the boy should have looked both ways, but Jimmy Grayson was twenty miles per hour over the limit. You don't do 45 in one of Beloit's nicer residential areas. The prosecutor was going to recommend a fine (paid by parents) and strict probation—two years in the juvenile hoosegow eminently suspended and maybe 200 hours of community service ridding Beloit's finer streets of strewn paper cups, some of which might well have been mine. But he needed recommendations, and who better than Beloit's still revered general of gridiron glory?

"I always said, both when I did Desert Storm and when we played Janesville Parker, you got to kill." I could tell we were in for a locker room talk, when we just wanted a kind and extenuating word about reckless Jimmy Grayson. "Of course it meant different things in Storm as opposed to the local stadium. We had guns in Storm. You don't have guns against Parker or Craig. But the idea's the same: you go in there trying to destroy. Well, that's what I told my platoon in Kuwait, and that's what I told my kids. I think that's good. You got a job to do: win. But after it's over you become a gentle soul. You only kill when you're supposed to. After that, you shake hands and buy somebody a Gatorade. That's my philosophy."

I had renewed vigor, thanks to the nap and the Taster's Choice (no Folger's; they make lousy powdered coffee). Roger was a bit nonplussed. I decided to treat this speech of Coach Duvall's as though it was the very soul of logic. What did I have to lose? No answers, please.

"But you don't think Jimmy was trying to *kill* this little kid, right, Coach?"

The coach had a slow and shouting way of talking. He considered his words with care; sort of a less intelligent guy's idea of what a really smart person would sound like. "Oh, no. I didn't mean that at all. What did I mean? Oh, I know. I meant that I wish I could have coached Jimmy in football. He's a little undersized, and I've retired. But I've known this kid and his parents all their lives. They've been right here next door. Jimmy's dad's gone a lot. He sells medical supplies, nitrogen tanks or something. But they're good people. And if Jimmy had had me as his coach, well, this would never have happened."

"No?"

"Absolutely not. You see, these kids have to get this killing out of their systems. You do that on the field."

At this point I sort of knew what Coach Duvall was trying to get at. He believed in what I'd learned to call "sublimation" back in my Beloit student days—this is a fourteen dollar word for the idea that if you get meanness out of your system in a harmless way you won't let it take over your life in a harmful one. This wasn't a bad theory. The trouble was this: Coach Duvall had left open the possibility that Jimmy *was* trying to kill this little tike because…well, because he hadn't had the chance to kill anybody from Janesville Craig between the forty and fifty yard lines under Coach Duvall. This was not what the county lawyer was looking for: He wasn't going to be crazy about the idea that this kid should get a suspended sentence because he'd never had the chance to kill a Janesville tailback under the watchful whites of Killer Coach Duvall.

"But you'd say this is not a bad kid, right, Coach?" This was Roger, bringing us back to the main motion.

"He's not. He just made a mistake. I think he was in a hurry or something. That's what his mom told me. I've seen this kid grow up. When he was little he'd put his toy trucks through something he called a car wash. He hosed them down really good. This is not a bad kid."

"Well, I think that's really what we came to hear, Coach." This is what I loved about Rugged Roger. He didn't like to complicate things. I cursed my gift for logic. Here I was trying to help Coach Ellis Duvall make sense of life, which he obviously thought was mostly a football game or a battle against Saddam, when I had a bad cold and should have been saving my overweight and overwrought breath.

We bid the coach adieu and told him the Purple Knights would never be the same without him. He loved that and gave us his best toothy one. It was an ambiguous statement, but ambiguity was not Coach Ellis' thing.

In the car Roger disproved my idea that he didn't like to complicate things by going straight to complicating things. "Let's stop by Gloria Drabble's. She's only a third of a mile off. It's convenient as long as we're out here."

"Why?" Damn it! What a terrible burden logic had become for me! I simply couldn't find any reason whatever why we needed to do this. We'd visited with her twice. She gave us nothing specific other than the bottom of an unlabeled box. We'd visited with her estranged husband, who questioned us a lot more than we had questioned him. There was absolutely nothing to this. If there was anything to this pseudo-case, then nothing whatever made sense, and Coach Duvall would be coaching the Purple Knights next week in their season opener against the Fort Atkinson River Rats.

"I just want her to know that we had spoken with her husband. He seems in the clear, though if you ask me...."

"Roger, if you want to tell her you've spoken to her estranged husband, why don't you try carrier pigeon? I've got a cold. I want to take off early."

But by the time I'd made my case we were there. We curved around the winding entrance. "Why," I asked no one in particular, "would the Drabbles move out here? His business is mostly in Rockford. This is one of the nicer houses out here, but they could afford much better."

Roger said, "I checked. They're just renting this place. If you ask me, they settled here so that Gloria, Mrs. Drabble, could keep taking occasional classes at the college."

"Oh." Well, Roger was up on his Drabbles, even if he needed a little help with his logic. Or so then I thought.

We approached the burnished oaken door, just past the neo-Doric wooden pillars that held up the fancy overhang of metal storks and sparrows in frozen flight. We rang the big brass doorbell, looking cheery with all the red roses painted around it. How can a doorbell be perky? But then I remembered Coach Duvall, who was a level man living in a level house; and after all, Gloria Drabble herself was a lady of jaunty sparkles. These people must build their dwellings to mirror themselves. I felt for a moment that I'd discovered a whole new theory, like Coach Ellis' notion of sublimation, though he'd never call it that or had even heard of it.

But my academic musings fell victim rudely to Roger, who said, "There's nobody around. Look at the mail box!"

I did. It was a big, cavernous rectangle, made of bright yellow-painted steel (more of Gloria's high spirits?). Inside it, sticking up in all its telltale wonder, was a six-inch box of Macy's Frango Mints. The heavy lid pressed down upon it like a crown of thorns.

PART THREE: THE SHOOTER

20: Tributaries

"Don't touch that!" shouted Roger to me. Why did he say that? I wasn't going to touch the box of Frango Mints. I wouldn't have touched the box of Frango Mints even if they were still put out by Marshall Fields. I wouldn't have touched them even if my big appetite was a Cat 4 hurricane. Why would I? I almost expected him to say, "They could be evidence." Evidence of what?

The bad cold had made a comeback. It had been putting points on the board all afternoon. Coach Ellis might say I was in danger of losing the game, despite my big second quarter nap with Dez on my gut. I suddenly realized that I'd been wiping mucous off my lip during the whole rollicking interview with Coach Ellis, and I hoped the great coach was not a germophobe. I knew he feared logic. How about bacteria?

Bacteria can kill.

I told Roger I just wanted to get back to the station, get in my pathetic little Nissan, and head home early. Oh, I sort of knew that he'd think this Frango thing was a big deal. Andrew Drabble had mentioned Frango Mints, and now here they were in the mailbox of the alienated Gloria, who wasn't at home, or so it seemed; and ergo, Andrew must have visited her with the mints as what, a peace offering, and had stopped by. Maybe. Maybe not. Maybe it was just the Frango Mints door-to-door salesman leaving a sample. I knew better than that. OK, so Andrew may have stopped by. Can a man not visit his wife?

But it was clear that Roger was somewhere between thrilled and seething. He was following his instinct again, and I was following my logic again. Well, that's how it appeared at the time. I wondered, not just then but often, if my college boy course in logic had turned me into somebody who lacked intuition for everything except one of Marie Callender's Chili Pot Pies. Had it turned me into a dullard? I was certainly somewhat repulsive to look at. Roger was all instinct and good looks—there was a feral quality to him; a Hollywood leading man type. This was my partner, and he had a sexy babe as a wife whose short hair-do got me to massage myself and maybe, what, brought out what my late and melancholy brother might have called my "Haitian tendencies." What? I had a bad cold. I was swooning. I was tired of trying to make sense of the world.

Roger was sure he made sense of the world: Mary was an affront to his professional ambitions and manhood; Andrew Drabble was guilty of something, if only of leaving Frango mints upside down in a steel trap mailbox; and (perhaps) Coach Ellis Duvall was just trying to be helpful when he was doing his failed psychologist routine. Not me. I had no idea what made sense any more, other than that I needed like fourteen hours sleep starting about an hour ago.

So Roger drove while I sat back and semi-snoozed. He had to wake me up when we got to the station. I know he was disappointed that we didn't talk about the telltale sign of the mints. I saw nothing improper, but then I'm a fat guy with a bad case of influenza and logic.

I went home. The crappy furniture and long Goodwill couch looked like Paradise. Here was a bed. Here I could recline. I didn't bother to eat anything, so you know I was sick. Dez seemed puzzled because she and I always dined together. She brushed up against my knuckles. Oh, yeah: one Fancy Feast coming right up, Madam. Dez didn't care about my germs.

Two Sudafeds, and although they were uppers (Jimmy and Julia had no doubt included them in their witches' brew) I went into the deepest fathoms of slumber. By now it was so early autumn that the darkness would come by 8. This comforted me. I liked the idea of enveloping black. It was my new blanket. Dez curled at my head. I needed to wash my hair. She didn't care. I told her I'd get her various reports from the town a little later. For now I was on sick leave.

When the phone rang six or so hours later I first couldn't believe it. This, I thought, can't be happening to me, first because no one would really need to ring me and second because no one should be ringing me. Did not the whole world know that I was desperately ill? Could not the world respect the narcissism of the sick?

Dez fled in a mad scamper. I stumbled to the other side of the room. I picked up. It was Baxter. Suddenly I thought about his ramrod straight posture and his pseudo-principled demeanor. Was he a Scoutmaster telling me to get my fat ass up and build a fire? I hated him for a second.

"Jeremy. We've got a man down. I need all personnel now. That includes you. Get over here right away. And before you ask, there's no overtime. You're salaried, got it?"

Why would Charlie think I'd even think about overtime? It was clear: he was agitated, angry, wasn't thinking straight. Can't anyone in this department think straight? And who was this "man down" and where was he? Had he been shot? It surely sounded like it. He wasn't poisoned with cyanide laced Godiva chocolates?

"Where? What man?"

"It's the Drabble place off Shopiere Road. You know it. You and Webb have been out there often enough. Get here!"

"Who's down? How?"

"Get here! I've got so much food on my plate, Dropsky, that even you couldn't handle it all. Just get out here. We've got half the cops in Beloit here already." Click.

Do phones even click any more when people hang up? The voice just vanishes, right?

I didn't get dressed and drive out there so much as floated out there. In fact, if I'd taken the cold med that makes you drowsy I'd have never made it. I was going on fumes. In one of the training courses Roger and I took they told us that after an adrenaline rush you get ravenous. I recalled this and noted I had no appetite as I headed across the river, veered a sharp north, passed by the old Catholic high school (now shuttered), and by the idle gas stations where lonely attendants must have been reading tabloids, and glared ironically at Our Lady of the Assumption's sprawling church complex and on out past the more clotted residential section of the Golden Ghetto and finally to the relatively isolated Drabble place, set smartly and snobbishly back from the road. At night it looked bigger. Cop cars were everywhere. There was an ambulance. Red lights circled as though high on Jim and Julie's stuff. Everything conspired to light up Gloria Drabble's domicile, whose adobe brick gave it the ambience of a local castle, even though I knew it was just a slightly more commodious than usual ranch house.

Please understand that I was still loopy. It occurred to me that all the lights were just attending a party to celebrate—what?—Gloria's having gotten an A in basket weaving or viola at Beloit College or Andrew's having landed a contract to build the new addition to the school for the blind in Janesville or the deaf in Delavan. Who was down? Had little Jimmy Grayson run over Gloria? But Charlie Baxter said a man was down.

Some of this now is a blur. But I remember winding my way through all the cars and the uniforms in an outside air fast becoming nippy, and watching out of the side of my eye as my distinguished colleagues were whisking Gloria out of the house to a squad car. One of the uniforms was skinny Jenny Dobbs; figures they'd have a woman to comfort and maybe later question a woman. Jenny stooped badly as though she was trying to hide her nose, which God had pinched badly. She was very bright; wanted to make detective; taller than I was by an inch. She'd played center at Memorial High. Now she tacitly steered Mrs. Drabble to some mobile shelter where she could forget about all this, whatever *this* was. Jenny said something to Gloria, likely something like you'll feel better when we get you out of here.

There's nothing like a little trauma to bring out the bromides.

Eventually I got into the house. I realized that I'd never really been able to explore the whole house, just the living room and the bedroom outside of which was found the notorious, and to my mind notoriously insignificant, box bottom. But now, as I wandered from room to room, crowded with techs and uniforms and a few other guys wearing whatever they could find to put on late in the evening on short notice, I saw that the place was fairly vast. There were four bedrooms, three baths (two full), a dining room, a sunroom, a finely cemented deck. This put my living room, kitchen, one bath, two bedrooms, and a stony weedy back yard to shame. But I had Dez while Gloria had this insufferable Persian who never reported anything of interest. That squared things.

I had no notion of where the Persian was at that point in time, and I still don't have any. She or he was deleted from my file, but please know: plenty of other subsequent things in this matter will never be deleted until I die off and not even then if "they" ever figure out how to upload my brain to zeroes and ones.

Finally, in the sunroom I found Charlie. He'd made this room his sort of unofficial office at the scene. This was central headquarters on this fledgling fall night in the Golden Ghetto, Crime Division. Or was it a crime? It was just a "man down," wasn't it? Charlie looked up at me when I entered. I always knew he thought I was out of shape and an investigating cop because of my brains and not my brawn. Charlie accepted that this was the new way. He didn't like it. He looked perturbed with me. The sunroom seemed wasted without any sun outside. It also seemed extremely indecorous, if you ask me, as a temporary office for Charlie Baxter, like a local K-Mart manager trying to find himself in Palm Springs. He rocked back and forth on his heels. He was in a fury. He had some forensics guys back there. He had a coroner back there. He had a uniform that he was shouting at, though I arrived a bit late to ever see what that was all about. He told me it was time I got there. He asked me why I was late. I wanted to be logical and say, "Because I just arrived," but Charlie was in no mood for my games. He had been asking questions—that was clear—but not so much asking them as vomiting them out.

I saw before me a very tall man extremely overwrought. I wondered if Charlie too had once played center for Memorial High basketball. It seemed such a frivolous thought under the circumstances. But when you don't know what the circumstances are, what else do you have left but frivolity?

"Look, Charlie. You can yell at me and then put me in the play. Or you can put me in the play and then yell at me. Or you can yell at me and then put me in the play and then yell at me some more. Sounds like you want to do the last. What's going on here? Take it from the top."

"There's been a shooting, Dropsky. A man is dead. I don't have time to get into details with you right now. I just called you out here because with this sort of thing you never know what the personnel needs are going to be. If you hurry you can see our dead friend. The ambulance is a hearse now, but it hasn't left yet, I don't think. But then what in hell do I know?"

I wended my way out, past the glassy tables (which were starting to make the whole place seem like a funhouse under the circumstances) and hefty maple chests of drawers and modernistic canopied beds (is that Victorian Revival or something?), and out the front door; past the bright bloody red-framed brass doorbell and the sunny steel deposit box for all important missives—and I headed for the back of the ambulance. Of course it was impossible not to notice that there was yellow crime scene tape blocking off the living room except for the scene of crime boys and girls with their sickly light blue coveralls and paper shoes, rustling about like dead leaves on a warmish night in November. May I unzip, I asked the EMS guy, a ruddy chap with a weasel face and unpolished brass hair. He said he didn't know why not; I was a cop; no evidence would be disturbed by a little unzipping— was he trying to make a dirty joke?

I decided to become lavish in my unzipping. I don't get to unzip other beings very often. It was Andrew Drabble. Somebody had closed his eyes for him. He who was little-big in life was just little in death. He'd probably stopped a bullet. The blood down the electric blue dress shirt was a red lake, a big splotch, but then, as though by some sort of geological miracle, it had spawned maybe eight or nine little red tributaries. They were helter-skelter. He had taken one in the heart. It wouldn't have taken him long to doze away forever. His small face was pasty white. Faces will do that when they don't get their regular diet of locomotive blood.

He looked so tiny, so utterly incompetent to deal with a well-aimed little missile at two hundred miles an hour. All that knowledge and hustle and arrogance: made to cease by just a teeny well-powdered pellet shot at a sufficiently high rate of speed. It should take more to kill a great man, but it doesn't.

I zipped him up again as though I were performing some sort of rite and wished the Weasel Man good luck. Good luck with what? I think in the presence of the dead you just sort of bond with the oddest people over life's fragility. I'd just been glued to a weasel, and we were stuck together for a moment by our mutual banalities.

I stumbled back into the house to seek out Baxter and find out if he wanted me to do anything; if he had anything for me to do; if he had just called me out there to scapegoat.

I found him in the sunroom again. He was still trying to piece together what had gone down. Something had gone down besides just a man; this man Andrew Drabble. Had Gloria shot him? Were they struggling over who got to eat the last Frango Mint?

Baxter looked up at me. "Sorry, Jeremy. I've been diddled out of my mind with this whole thing. I recall now why I wanted you here. You've got a job to do. Go out to the patio and you'll find it."

"What am I looking for?"

"You'll find it. And I want you to remember it; remember it all. Got your notebook?"

"Never without it, Captain."

"Go!"

I turned right out of the sunroom, ambled through the cozy den with the mock fireplace in the stony faux rustic corner, and found the back door. The deck was thoroughly concrete, even the bannisters. This was the solid rock. It even put the old Presby Church on Public Avenue to shame. There was no wood to rot here. Transience would have no chance to triumph. The outdoor lights soaked this patio, which had settled imperviously, as though it were doing a fair imitation of a cliff. At the end, on the steps down to the yard, sat a guy with a blanket around him. He was shivering, but it wasn't that cold. I recognized him from the back. I'd know the other side of that head anywhere.

It was Roger.

He heard my approach. He turned half way round to greet me.

"Hello, Jeremy. Thanks for coming. I'm the shooter."

21: Drip-Dried Condition

If this story had been in some sentimental novel about Platonic friendship, Roger and I would have sat on the back of Gloria Drabble's deck, under the stars, and re-told our life stories to one another. But there weren't any stars—it was a cloudy night. And this was now an official police matter. It was, by the way, only when I finally left the Drabble premises that I noticed the deep purple Lexus, the nearest car around to the front door. That must have been, I decided, the late Andrew's, and I was right.

It was a jumble: the late hour, the suddenly dead man, Roger's confession (which Charlie Baxter already knew about), Gloria's traumatic exit, the contradictory directions given to the scene of crime team. I've got to admit that, after initially bumping around like a blind terrier, the SOC boys and girls recovered nicely and picked up some useful information. By the time I left, my cold Nissan, sitting by patiently to whisk me back to some sort of real, the ambulance, a.k.a. hearse, had already departed.

Perching on the back stoop with Roger and having a heart-to-heart wasn't precisely what you'd call good police procedure. There is no book in which that's allowed, unless it's by some crime novelist. So of course after hearing Roger say that he had shot Andrew Drabble to that great construction site in the heavens, I told him right away that we'd have to talk more down at headquarters.

Why did Charlie send me back there? He knew what Roger would say. He knew Roger was hunkered down back there. He knew, or I like to think he knew, that I would immediately turn this whole thing into a formal interview with the microphones and recorders on. Charlie had asked me before I ever went back there if I had my notebook, but surely this was a ruse, though why he pulled it I still don't know. I never asked Charlie, but my guess is that he was anxious to put some sort of human factor into what had become a pretty weird night, and so he sent me to the back yard so that Roger would know that his dear old partner was on the scene, regardless of what had happened. Well, yeah, his dear old partner was on the scene, but the business Roger and I were in was investigation of crimes or potential crimes. So my little visit with the man who called himself "the shooter" would have brought all the comfort that one of Gloria's expensive nail files would have supplied to a cuticle that wanted to stay sharp.

Charlie said we were all going to get a few hours' sleep before we commenced with this thing. Roger would go back to the station and rest on a cot, and some of the night shift would watch over him, and the emergency room of Beloit Memorial had been alerted that a cop might need some medical attention for his mental state. Mrs. Andrew Drabble would go to the motel room of her choice (she took the Beloit Inn on Pleasant). We would all gather back at headquarters by no later than 10 A.M. We would do this systematically. We would do interviews. We would get a forensic report. We would confer with the District Attorney. Of course by 7 A.M. the city manager and council members had all been alerted that a little difficulty might be forming, though it wasn't entirely clear how much or for whom. The local papers,

Beloit *Daily News* and Janesville *Gazette*, were already nosy. They got people listening to police scanners who call them up. Rockford would come calling, too—hell, especially Rockford: Andrew lived and worked there. He was even what you might call integral to the local economy.

Charlie decided we would talk with Mrs. Drabble first, in order to find out what, in Charlie's words, "the eternal hell happened out there." Charlie thought he knew. He was into rooting for his guys. Me, I'm enough of a college near-grad to know what Sherlock Holmes said about the capital error of drawing conclusions in advance of the facts. Pardon me if I've made this point before. Charlie was not a reader. He was more of a listener, maybe: let's say he liked Tammy Wynette's "Stand By Your Man" with Man = One Of *My* Men.

Tell the truth, I theorize now that Charlie really wanted to hear from Roger first: get his story on the record as a kind of first-strike against Gloria's (Andrew would be having nothing to say). But Charlie also knew that you hear from the witnesses before you hear from the gunner. I admire Charlie for this. He wanted to stand by Roger, but he was a cop first. Well, in the end he was.

I'd already described Gloria Drabble as a kind of cheerleader, but that's not quite right. High school cheerleaders fake their enthusiasm. So would you if you had to lead the same yells fifty times a night. Nah. Gloria's cheer was more genuine. It was more substantial. This was the joy of a 40 something woman who had faced enough things not to cheer about but had continued her yells for Life's Team after all. She had a more earned optimism.

Now she was the Titanic if someone had managed to dredge it up. She'd had a head-on crash. In effect, the carburetor was scattered on the side of the road. Yet somehow the engine kept running. Pardon the comparison. It's forced. But I'm still trying to make sense of this thing. Or maybe I should say that once I *did* make sense of this thing, then I *really* needed to make sense of this thing. But I'm getting ahead of myself.

When I say the engine was still running, I mean she maintained a kind of liveliness. She was telling us about a tragedy, and yet she still had a latent bubbliness about her. I don't mean bubble-headed. I'm talking about champagne here; something classy like Cook's or Korbel's. Life was still a wonder somehow, and even if nothing but watery tears kept descending from her face, you got the idea that she would insist, in some tacit way, that implicit enthusiasm about life was justified after all. You had the impression that by this time next week Mrs. Drabble would agree with the statement that life was yet a marvelous thing in the teeth of of it all. It was like this: The willow weeps, but my, isn't it an interesting tree? *My husband is dead. I've been stuck in the horror. The sun still shines, and isn't it a nice morning? I can't stop crying, but then shirts cry too if they're drip-dried and then they're ready to wear to the party.*

She did cry and cry through that interview. This was hardly fakery. She had to stop often to catch her breath and force herself to continue. She choked out fragments of testimony so that several times we had to summarize it for her to see if this was what she was saying. Most of the time she agreed: it was. This was about the size of it, she sobbed: she stared at this repulsive pile of demonic dread, of agonizing panic, and yet—and this is ineffable and nonsensical, I know—what a world to afford such harrowing stimulus as this. It was strange. She was strange.

She was also sincere. We were sure of that. In fact, the gladness lurking in her horrible tale made it all the more convincing. This was Gloria Drabble, whose inner cheerleader would not yet surrender even in the face of this, this…thing.

She *would* get this right. Go, Team!

She wished she hadn't called Roger, but she had his card, and he had written down his mobile number on it. She'd have probably been all right even if he hadn't arrived. She wasn't sure of this, but she thought it likely. She didn't want to get him involved. She and Andrew might have worked out their troubles on their own. It's just that, well, she was frightened. She'd never told anyone before how emotionally abusive Andrew could be. He was a rich man, a successful one. He was used to being on the winning side of a 1-0 vote, with her casting the null ballot. She had asked for space. She was sure she wasn't what he wanted. He'd told people, she'd heard, that she was just insecure. But she *wasn't* insecure, she said. She was mistreated. Andrew had told her she was a bore; a goody-two-shoes; a *Good Housekeeping* whore. He was tired of her. He would see others. But she was not to cast him off. She was his. So when he got out to Shopiere Road last night he told her: He married her, and she was not to give the world the impression that she had kicked him out—that he could *be* kicked out. He'd put up with it for some months. But now he was done. He'd been rejected, humbled enough. She was to move to Rockford with him and do it now. They would go to parties and dinners. She would entertain clients. Andrew Drabble was not to be known as a man who could keep his awful wedded wife. Viola lessons were optional.

"Did he ever harm you physically?" asked Charlie.

"Never. But he made me feel awful about myself. He took liberties with my head, my soul." This was one of her more articulate sentences.

"But you thought he might harm you last night?"

"He said he would. He phoned me. He said he was halfway to Beloit. He said this time I could yield to his fists or his cock. I could choose. He was bonkers."

"And that's why you called Roger?"

"Yes."

"Why not call 911?"

"I should have. But I'd kept Officer Webb and Dropsky's cards right by my bed. I knew where they were. They'd been out to the house. Somehow I thought of them as my protectors. I messed up. I know that."

"Why not call Sergeant Dropsky?"

"Officer Webb's was the card on top."

I jumped in. "This is maybe beside the point now. But do you think it was your husband who was prowling around your house? Did he leave you a box of Frango Mints recently? We saw them in your mailbox late yesterday afternoon. Sergeant Webb suggested we look in on you."

"Yes, I assume it was Andrew who left me the mints. He knew I loved them. I don't know when he left them. I found them when I came in from shopping at Schnuck's in Roscoe. Andrew never said anything about them after he, you know, after he arrived."

"And this was what time?"

"Early. Or late. I'd say around 1 in the morning. He never said anything about the candy."

"Were the Frango Mints, do you think, a sign of anything? A message?"

"I think so. I think he showed up earlier with a peace offering. I wasn't there. He left the candy. Then for some reason he went back to Rockford and started to stew, and that's when he called me to say he was on his way for a showdown about the future of our marriage."

I thought briefly that marriage seemed to me an odd institution. *You can take my mints or you can take my fists. You choose.* And you think I'm nuts because I'm a bachelor with a talking cat.

"So what happened once he arrived, and how long was he there before Sergeant Webb arrived?"

"Sergeant Webb arrived about maybe three, four, five minutes after Andrew banged on the door and made me let him in?"

"Did he really *make* you let him in?"

"I was afraid of what he'd do if I didn't."

"So you called Sergeant Webb about, what, ten minutes before your husband arrived?"

"Maybe not quite ten. I can't say. Ten seems a little long."

"We'll get a more precise timeline down later," Charlie said, sounding a bit admonitory.

"So then what exactly happened once Mr. Drabble entered your residence?" I was trying to use neutral cop language.

"He came in yelling. He was in a fury. He said I'd hurt him and now he was going to hurt me. He said I was just a legal call girl; *his* legal call girl. He said he could easily do better but he didn't want clients to think he was an asshole, so he was going to keep me. I was going to come back to him. He said old clients had liked me, and he wanted to keep them. He said they must be stupid to like me. But I belonged to him, and we were going to put up appearances together. He'd decided. He'd decided I was his. He said I could do my no-talent routine just as well in Rockford as in Beloit. He said I was no good in bed and likely no good at viola. I've only had a few lessons. But there were beds in Rockford and viola lessons in Rockford, and that's where we were going to live, and then...."

Wailing hiccups and then: "he ran into the kitchen and he came back with one of the butcher knives and he told me he'd bought this for me because I'd asked for it, for just this one. It's an expensive Wusthof; maybe ten inches long. He got about two feet away and backed me into a corner and circled it around in his hand one way and then the other.....right to left and otherwise and maybe up and down, but I forget...and he asked me if I'd like to use this as my viola bow and he wondered if that would work because it would cut the strings and there'll be no more viola lessons and he asked me if I wanted him to show me how sharp it was and if he thought him using this would improve my performance in bed."

"How close did he come to stabbing you? Was he going to do that?"

"I don't know. I think he might have started to lunge at me but I don't know. But I think so. He never got the chance, you see."

"And Sergeant Webb—why did he come right in without knocking? Or did he knock?"

"I don't think so. He knew I was frightened. He might have heard me. I was in hysterics. I can't imagine I wasn't making noise. You'll need to ask him."

"And when he got there, did he see your husband brandishing the butcher knife?"

"Yes, and I do believe he told him to drop it."

"And what did your husband do? What did he say?"

"He said a profanity and asked Sergeant Webb who he was and what was he doing in his house? He screamed at Sergeant Webb."

"Your husband had met Sergeat Webb before, in Rockford. Why would he ask Sergeant Webb who he was/"

"I don't know. He did, though."

"But your husband wasn't facing you when he was shot. Did he still have the knife in his hand?"

"Oh, oh, yes, he did. He never gave it up until he fell from the bullet."

"Did Sergeant Webb ask him to drop it?"

"I'm not certain, but I'm pretty sure he did. This is a blur."

"Your husband didn't drop it."

"No, as I said, not until he was shot."

"But your husband had his back to you when he was shot?"

"Yes. But I think (I can't be sure) when Sergeant Webb arrived Andrew had planted his two feet and was ready to turn around and stab me."

"Are you sure about that? Did Sergeant Webb see this?"

"Not sure, but I think Andrew was ready to lunge and I think Sergeant Webb witnessed this."

"You believe he witnessed this right before he shot your husband, but your husband was no longer lunging at you with the knife when Sergeant Webb shot him? He was facing Sergeant Webb?"

Her face was a puffy mask. She tried to smile, an emaciated glow behind a dominant bruised cloud. A faint gladdening wished to whisper something; anything.

"Yes. I think that's what happened. I really do."

"So are you suggesting that your husband was about ready to turn back around and stab you?"

"I don't know. I think so. But that must have been what Sergeant Webb thought because, well, you know, he fired his weapon at Andrew, who wouldn't drop the knife."

"But how did your husband's body end up with his head draped over the back of the big easy chair?"

"I think...I think Andrew after he was shot was trying to collapse in that chair but didn't have enough life left to turn around and sit in it. He got in the chair face first and ended up with his head sort of, well, dangling over the back of it."

Actually, I'd say, from the reports I read, that Andrew Drabble's poor mini-head was *bent* over the back of the giant lounge chair. It was bent. He was found bent dead in Beloit.

22: Trunky Business

We had Roger in next, but between interviews Charlie had gotten an updated report from the scene of crime people. He was startled by what they told him, but he didn't tell anyone. He didn't tell me. So I went into the *q & a* with Roger without it.

Roger's face looked almost as ravaged as Gloria Drabble's, except that Roger had no hidden reserves of sunshine. Here's a good-looking guy, an Adonis by our Midwestern standards, but he looked twenty-five years older, as though this whole thing had done overnight what generally you'd expect years of drinking and smoking and angering to do. It was like Roger knew that he'd aged, and that was part of the reason for a glumness so black that the lights had not only gone out but would never come on again except maybe at about 25 watts. I looked at him and thought that the power had gone out at 3 A.M. in January and all you had to look forward to was the sun coming up (but probably behind the clouds) and then lowering the shades again by early afternoon and this was the rest of your frigid life. As it turns out, this description was as melodramatic as it was wrong.

Well, I thought, in my most partisan pro-Mary moment yet, you wanted to be a hero, so this is what you get. Take extra care with what you most desire.

But my job was to help get the facts, so I tried to do that. Charlie took the lead and started at the start—where else?

"So where were you when you got this call from Mrs. Drabble. We know when you got it. We have your phone. But where were you?"

"Uh, you know Mary and I are split, right? I'm not living there. I'd rented a room downtown, above one of the old gift shops on Grand. I was there."

"And what did she say?"

"She said her husband was on his way to her house. She said he was mad and she was afraid of him. She'd been jittery for a while now about prowlers. She was upset. She asked me to drop over. She wanted somebody else there."

"Why'd she call you?"

"You'd have to ask her. You probably have. I assume she had my number from the cards Jeremy here and I left with her. She knew me. She knew I was police. That's all I can think."

"Did she say that Mr. Drabble had a gun?"

"No."

"Did you think he did or might?"

"I wasn't thinking about that especially."

"Didn't it cross your mind? You took your piece with you."

"I always do that on police business."

"Didn't you ever think, he might have a gun?"

"I must have. I might have. I can't say for sure."

"What did you expect to do there? What did you expect to find? When did she say Mr. Drabble would arrive? Why didn't you call for back-up?"

"She didn't say. She said he was on his way. She said she thought he was near. She just wanted someone else to be there, OK? I didn't want to bother back-up. This didn't seem to justify it."

At this point Roger got surly. It passed off quickly, and I thought he had gone snarly because he had this sense of facing some gusher of cyanide overdose all alone and thought he might feel better if he at least shook his fist at it, as though that would help.

"I'm sorry, buddy," I said. "We have to get this right. You killed an important guy, and he wasn't armed. We're not against you here."

"OK." He seemed resigned to what he didn't want to be resigned to. "I didn't really know what to expect. Probably I thought this was going to be a domestic. I'd mediate and go home, all right?"

"When you drove up did you see Mr. Drabble's Lexus?"

"Of course."

"So you knew he was there."

"I knew unless somebody else with a Lexus was visiting."

"You knew him by sight?"

"Yes, but that wouldn't have made any difference."

"What do you mean by that?"

"I mean that it could have been—OK, goddamned Mother Theresa holding that butcher knife."

Roger was excitedly depressed. I didn't think for a moment that he'd have shot Mother Teresa holding a butcher knife. My pesky logic kept getting in the way. This is my partner we're talking out. This is the man who of all men justly deserves being found justifiably homicidal. He just does. He just did, OK? He talked me out of a suicide mission once. I wasn't planning to wave the white flag on this concept of what benefit Roger deserved any time soon. I wasn't *planning* to.

"Now Roger—Sergeant Webb—we get to the nub of this thing," said Charlie. "You drive from downtown Beloit way out to Shopiere. That's about ten minutes. That all checks out with the timeline we've documented. No problems. But now you drive up. What do you hear? What do you see?"

"I hear Mrs. Drabble screaming *no*. I hear her screaming no two or three times."

"And? How clear did you hear it?"

"Clear enough to know what the word was; to know she was in trouble; to know it was her. What else?"

Roger sounded like some seedy barfly making his last stand, telling the world why he'd chosen to take a nightly habitual swim in the perfect Johnny Walker Black. I mean, he was ransacked and looted. You could see it the eyes, which seemed reduced to a couple of piss holes, and in the temples that pulsated like some devouring lava was about to pop up and have us all for supper. Roger looked done for life.

I thought he was moving into shadows, and that the motion itself was the only truth he had left.

"OK. That's what you heard. Now you tried the front door, right?"

"I tried the front door."

"And it was unlocked?"

"Yes."

"What would you have done if it hadn't been?"

"I don't know. Likely shot the lock. What difference does that make? It was unlocked."

"Were all the lights on in the living room?"

"They were on enough so that I could see clear. I don't know beyond that."

"Now when you got into the room Mr. Drabble had his back to you?"

"Yeah. I think it took a moment for it to register to him that someone else was there."

"Why? Doesn't the door make a sound when it opens?"

"Maybe he was slow. Maybe he was focused on what he was doing."

"He turned all the way around to face you?"

"Maybe three quarters. He didn't seem to recognize me. He asked me what I was doing there. He didn't seem to know who I was."

"Did he brandish the butcher knife at you?"

"No. He told me to get out. I told him to drop the knife."

"What was Mrs. Drabble doing?"

"By the time I got here she had stopped gasping, stopped yelling. I wasn't paying much attention to her, though. I wanted him to drop the butcher knife. She was up against the wall. When

I arrived he was facing her with the knife. She had been saying no."

"How far were you from the two of them?"

"Maybe six feet. Maybe seven feet. Not sure."

"What did he do after he told you to get lost and you told him to drop it?"

"He was facing me with maybe three quarters of his body. He got on the balls of his feet. He didn't say anything. I know he was about to turn back to her. I think he thought by telling me to leave he'd gotten rid of me. I didn't matter any more. I didn't count. He was about to turn full body back to her with this knife. I pulled my Glock from my inside jacket pocket. It was ready to go. I dropped him."

"You shot a man facing you three quarters?"

"Yes, I did. This was what I needed to do. I had to save Mrs. Drabble."

"Couldn't you have shot the knife out of his hand?"

"I think I might have been aiming to do that. He didn't stand still. But I needed to save Mrs. Drabble. She was in danger."

"You weren't trying to kill him?"

"I was trying to stop him. I needed to do that."

"We searched the trunk of Mr. Andrew Drabble's car," said Charlie. "It wasn't a huge priority, but you know—from experience—that you have to do everything."

"Yeah, " said Roger.

"Yeah?" I said. My "yeah" had a question mark at the end of it. Why was Charlie bringing this up?

"It was loaded with supplies of Sudafed and lithium batteries," said Charlie. "Mr. Drabble's Lexus trunk was full of that stuff."

Roger looked up with the faint flicker of a man who just might have heard about the possibility of a reprieve, a terminal cancer patient whose doctor told him he'd somehow misread the tests. He wasn't looking fifty-five any more. He was forty-five all of a sudden, maybe going on thirty.

PART FOUR: THE MISSION

23: John Candy and Chris Farley Are Dead

Of course Charlie was right that everything had to be pinned down. Roger had shot a man without a gun. His wife said that she felt threatened by this man, but he didn't have a gun. He had a butcher knife, but he'd not cut her with his knife, nary a hair on her lively and wholesome if weeping head had been touched. Roger said he had tried to shoot this man's arm, the one holding the knife, but that he had turned suddenly, presumably to get back to his goal of treating Gloria as viola strings, so of course Roger had missed the arm and hit the heart. Death came before you could say, "Andrew Drabble had it coming to him." Meanwhile, our boys had finally gotten around to searching Mr. Drabble's Lexus, which was a big car for a tiny but demanding and overbearing man, and found meth materials. This was quite the recipe for trouble, and I don't just mean the nice red liquid decongestant and the lithium strips, which had as yet not been pried apart from the batteries.

Now there had never been anything to connect Mr. Andrew Drabble with meth. We had nothing on him buying it or selling it or using it or distributing it or hiding it or having sex with it. Rockford had nothing of this sort of evidence either. Andrew Drabble was maybe a rather nasty little guy, but then they tend to be in the construction business. He was cocky and liked to run the conversation, but then he'd not gotten successful by standing in the corner and looking at the wall while nibbling on Frango Mints. No one succeeds that way. There had never been any sign that he'd tried to cheat anybody with shoddy materials or breaches of contract. There was no reason to think that he'd ever need and want—need or want—to go into the illegal drug biz.

Julia and James, though, having read of this find in Andrew's trunk, quickly came out of bail obscurity to say that maybe, just maybe, Mr. Drabble, the rather non-dearly departed, had been the Mr. Big of whom they spoke. No doubt their information about Andrew had been buttressed by the private detectives hired by their now anxious rich parents. Their lawyers from Janesville proffered that J&J had good reason to think this because they'd been told (by whom was left fuzzy) that after they passed a certain sales mark "the little man from Rockford" would give them a heap big bonus. If you ask me, in any more routine matter we'd have dismissed this stuff. It was all wren droppings and it smelled bad. There was nothing to it, and I think to this day that Charlie Baxter and the D.A. knew there was nothing to it.

This was just a couple of spoiled and wayward kids trying to get out of something. They'd said they might, just might, give us Mr. Big in exchange for a favor, and now they were sort of, kind of, maybe, just maybe, doing it. They were peddling rumors from unknown sources. Prosecution wasn't overly curious about these sources. Why?

Well, here again I have my own ideas. Andrew Drabble in death had very few sponsors. He had a construction company with several regular and salaried employees. But most of what he did he outsourced. His parents were long dead, and the only sister he had lived in Prescott, Arizona, and had never liked her little bro much. She didn't attend the services, which were strictly graveside. His regular workers would need to find new jobs, because although Gloria would inherit the company she had no way of knowing how to run it and would sell it out. Her thing was viola, not building volume. This, I thought, wasn't a bad payoff for a little adventure looking at a butcher knife. But I didn't much like Gloria. I liked Mary. I couldn't imagine Gloria going to Homecare Pharmacy to buy her Bounty towels. I imagined her looking to see if she could get those delivered, though I've got to admit that I know of no one in Beloit who does that kind of thing.

I digress. My point is that you may have sponsors in life, but do you have them in death? Andrew, once he became late, had few to none. He was a loner. He only had Gloria, and she was the one in whose company he had gotten himself shot dead. So when it came time for people to say nasty things about him for their own convenience there wasn't anyone around to stop them.

And in a way why wouldn't the county prosecution folks believe Julia and Jim? Hadn't this druggie matter been found in the trunk? And weren't J&J from a prominent, if prehistoric, Beloit family? Doesn't money still talk and assure that nobody who has it has to walk? Unlike Tiny Andy Drabble, JJ had sponsors, at least in their rancid lives. So the county attorneys accepted the proposition that James and Julia had "cooperated" with "possibly useful information" and reduced their sentences to time served and a 50 grand fine each. They found a plutocratic judge to approve. Their parents begrudgingly paid and no doubt told their hopeless kids to do something more legal the next time they wanted to take a fine trip. If I had been hired to tutor them, I'd have tried to organize them to learn how to hack, which is lawless but fairly hard to trace and really, really hurts people—sometimes even more than those cat litter crystals they were peddling to what they called, in self-defense, "young adults." Yeah, right. But web hacking would have taken brains, and I fear JJ's noggins were left over fried rutabaga by now.

Of course J&J were really bit players. The real issue was Roger. He was a cop, and the force wanted to protect him if they could. It helped that lith and Sudafed had been sleeping it off in the Lexus. To be sure, an autopsy revealed no traces of anything stronger than ibuprofen and a tiny amount of Chardonnay in old Andrew's corpse. But the idea was that a man who might be Mr. Little Big Man in the meth enterprise would also be a man who would cut his wife to viola ribbons. Note the phrase "might be." There was never any solid evidence that Andrew Drabble was ever any such thing. But hey, he *might be*, and someone who *might be* would surely butcher his spouse, right?

Roger had been in this town for nearly a decade. He was a bit of a hunk with a really nice smile. He never failed to do the right thing, like listen to Rose's embittered laments about Susan or make sure that he left no boulder unearthed to guarantee that decent Mrs. Gloria Drabble was all right. He wasn't like me, a blubbery logician ex-college boy. He was a movie star cop with instincts—the kind you see on TV. I mean, when you have to see cops for any reason you look for something to mitigate the poignancy. A cop in your life for nearly any reason is not good news. And so the ladies would think, "well, at least they sent me a good-looking one," and the guys would think, "now there's a rugged man I can respect." So Roger was a valuable commodity, or so he was thought to be. Beyond that, no police department wants to have it bruited about that their cops are irresponsible or crooked or even careless. So there was a lot riding on the idea that the Drabble business was a tragedy, yeah, but an entirely unpreventable one and that it would have been even worse if Gloria had been pierced in her deeply, squeaky clean heart—because she would have been innocent—and if good cop Roger's life had somehow been ruined via a long imposed holiday in Waupun or to wherever in the Badger State he would have been transported much against his raging will and in opposition to the rallying fury of the community he had served so well.

So Roger's story checked out. It had to check out. It was sad, but look at it another way: Roger was a hero. He had saved a life. He had killed a meth man armed with an instrument that was lawfully used only to slice flank steak that once was part of a dead cow's rump.

But it gets even better. Roger had told me he wanted to get a big break. Did he have it now? He received lots of local publicity, some regional acclaim, and even some national attention. Yeah, he was a little controversial. There was the usual gang of liberals who thought cops shot too quickly and asked about the consequences too late. But nobody with any regard for public safety listens to those old ladies in britches.

But it was even better. While the likes of overweight Jeremy Dropsky were skeptical that there ever was anything to the whole Drabble business—as I myself saw nothing but persiflage in all that business about Frango Mints and viola lessons—Roger followed his gut. He was right all along. Andrew Drabble was a crazed and possessive outlaw husband about to crack. Hell, he might even have been getting ready to *sell* crack. Thank goodness Sergeant Roger Webb had gotten there in time.

No charges against Roger Webb were ever filed, and the important people complimented him in public on his quick thinking and last minute salvation and going beyond the call of duty after hours.

In short—short is also my belated homage to Andy Drabble—Roger had found opportunity not just knocking but banging with happy fury on the door. He was a cop show hero. He had been right all along. The only question was who would play him in the movie? I even wondered who would play me. After all, Chris Farley was dead, and so was John Candy.

And who would play my beloved Mary? Would she even get a part?

24: Wants and Needs

It took Roger almost no time to capitalize on how everything came down. Andrew Drabble was likely a meth man, though exactly why or how was never lucid. I'd even venture to say that Andrew's meth was a myth. But look: according to public perception he was almost surely a dangerous and controlling husband, whose past, alleged mental abuse of ingenuous Gloria had finally boiled up into butcher knife rage. Julia and Jim were confirmed, sort of, in their myopic account of some Mr. Big somewhere, of whom they had heard but never seen. They couldn't even say who had told them that Mr. Big existed, but this was no matter. Finally, above all, Roger had, it was all but universally presumed, done his best. He had missed in his aim, but that's what happens when a little turd like Andrew can't decide where he wants to stand with his costly foot-long blade. Roger was a hero. He was cop show material. His big break had come. He wasn't going to let it come and go. He would grab it by the lapels first.

Charlie had placed him on continued administrative leave so that he could recover fully from the ordeal of being Popeye Policeman. So I had no partner for a long time, but then I got a partner, yet it wasn't Roger, since he had taken a job elsewhere. He'd come from Milwaukee and wanted to go back there. He had to settle for Aurora, which was now the second largest city in Illinois. He would go there as a lieutenant, mostly because the Aurora police department had been exposed as rife with fixing tickets and busting innocent heads. They needed a winsome heroic face. Roger was in. The Aurora media hailed his having been hired. It was a new day for the APD.

Everybody wanted to believe this whole thing. Well, nearly everybody, because I didn't want to believe it. I felt abandoned, for one thing. Roger had been my partner. I thought he valued our partnership. You can't blame a man for moving on, but he never even bothered to call from wherever he'd moved to. Somebody said that during his leave time he'd found a two-bedroom place near the college, just across from the gay pride house. Was Roger's place the Hero Pride House? Nope, for Roger re: me it was slam bam and thank you, ma'm. Not that I was in love with Roger, though he'd once saved my fat ass from Robert Boso's nickel .38. I was in love with Mary.

And that's the other thing. He had left Mary. He had shattered her soul. OK, that's melodramatic, but it's my melodrama. I would still say he hurt her very much. She too didn't even get a phone call, except from Roger's lawyer. Well, I loved Mary, and that's another reason I didn't necessarily want to buy Roger's story, which was what I used to call "that other melodrama," the forgotten Mary being the first one.

Even before Roger left for Aurora, when he was still licking his wounds on the road to celebrating his triumph, I looked in on Edith Earl. She was in forensics and scene of crime stuff. She was petite and sweet, feisty when needed, a bottle blond with dark roots and pasty face. She was neon white, not especially attractive, but she knew her work. Who am I, a ton of constabulary fun, to talk about attractive? She'd gotten a husband, and he was the best local plasterer around. Did he specialize in white? Yeah, likely.

"Yo, Edith. Question: Did you all take prints on Mr. Drabble's butcher knife?"

"Of course, Jeremy. Who do you think we are? What was the name of that Peter Sellers cop?"

"Inspector something or other French. Don't give me an old movie quiz. It doesn't become you. OK, so you took the prints. How many prints did you find?"

"One set."

"One set as in o-n-e? Didn't Mrs. Drabble say that was her butcher knife and that he'd gotten it from her kitchen counter?"

"I don't know, Jeremy. You detectives are supposed to keep track of the story. We just do the physical evidence, or have you forgotten that?"

"I haven't forgotten. One set. Got that. Might bother you again. I think the name of Peter Sellers' dumb detective was Inspector Closet. I could be wrong."

"That doesn't sound right."

"Nothing sounds right."

Cursed, Jeremy, be thy logic. That and calories are the great problems of my life, you see. After my victorious conversation with Edith Earl I celebrated with a full extra crispy with the Colonel, took the remainders home, and gave them to Dez and asked her what she made of just one set of prints, Andrew's, on that knife. I forget what she said, but I do recall that she thought it odd, too.

And then I got lucky with the Energizer AA lithium jobs, and with the Mucinex and Creomulsion remedies for those tickles in your throat, not to mention that roiling junk in your chest. It seems that they'd found those, too, along with Sudafed the Red-Nosed Snot-Clear, in Mr. Drabble's cavernous trunk. And with this one, the fifth time was a charm. I sort of figured that no one would want to make these purchases inconveniently, so the location of a hardware store next to a CVS in north Rockford was the key to all mythologies. I can still see the stooped and skinny little man with the withdrawn hairline and the powder blue coat telling me with a grin about how "yeah, I remember her. We called her the Shady Blonde after she left the second time. She bought six lithium batteries every time. If you tell me she was buying cough syrup next door, which I guess you are, then I'll have to say, Mister Sheriff that she was planning to electrocute Nyquil, whatever good that does. Older I get, less sense life makes."

Older and fatter and more logical I get, the more life does make sense, at least in a way. There's a little doom in that for me. Between my logic and Dez's nightly visits I see things I shouldn't see and don't want to see. But wait a minute! I must want to see them or I'd stop looking for them.

I wonder if that deteriorating powder blue Ace-is-the-place hardware man also sensed that there was a wig in the place and that as a handy hardware man all he had to do was yank it off. I don't think he saw any of this. Maybe that's why he works in a hardware store and I work in a cop shop.

And then there was a little visit with Professor Wilma Riddlehauer of Beloit College. She was glad to see me, Professor W was; thought I might be returning to class, maybe. Naw. I just wanted to get a consultation. I swore her to confidentiality and didn't much care if she kept her holy vow (as it turned out, she did). I showed her Roger's signed statement and asked her about a couple of spots. One of them she dismissed; said my brain was working overtime. Roger had said something like "I had just gotten here," which I took to mean that he'd been *there* (Mrs. Drabble's house) so often that he thought of it as a "here." I recalled how Joe the Mac's Tap barkeep had told Roger that he'd not seen him in a good long while—wasn't Roger with Gloria instead? Wilma shot that "here v. there" business down. "It could be a typo. You don't know it isn't. Even if he technically misspoke, he might have been going over the thing in his mind so much that *there* became *here*—it was very vivid to him."

But her inner Wittgenstein and mine were on the same skeptics' track when Roger said that, "I needed to shoot him." Professor W. said that if you look at that language with care you'll find that Roger is really using "needed" in order to mean "wanted," as in "I really needed to buy that sauna or that Acura. If Roger had meant that it was necessary to shoot Andrew in order to save little Gloria's life he'd have said, "I had to shoot him." Wilma thought that "needed" was a giveaway that Roger *wanted* to shoot Andrew, and so did I, and she congratulated me on my good eye and invited me once more to give up at least part of my life as a peace officer and return to the prospects of becoming a professor some day.

She also said that neither she nor I could be certain we were correct.

One thing I pondered repeatedly: at the end of this whole cruddy business we'll never know what Andrew Drabble was really like, but it wasn't hard to think that however much of an ass he was, he was never an abusive husband, had never touched that butcher knife except when Roger and Gloria put his dead hand on its elegant handle, and had been totally lured to the Golden Ghetto and set up and shot up. I wish I could have known the real Andrew Drabble. With him as the little squirrel and me as the great big elephant we might have been a great comedy team.

I thought that only Dez could tell me if I was right. If only the wee Dez had been there in those wee hours when wee Andrew Drabble showed up at that hefty ranch house he'd rented for his wonted bride, Dez could have given me an exact account. Dez Sez: that's what I needed to be sure I was right about what had gone down.

But then they'd sooner listen to Wittgenstein than listen to a cat. And Wittgenstein had been dead for nearly seventy years.

25: The Last Word He Spoke

Andrew Drabble wouldn't plausibly be the sole owner of the fingerprints on that butcher knife. He was the sole owner of lots of things but not that, not in any believable sense. That's what the physical evidence showed, though. And it gave away the show. Lizzie Borden was accused of killing her father and stepmother with an axe, and folks have been debating whether or not she really done it. Well, she did. She done it. How do I know? Because she told everyone that her stepmother had stepped away from the house to visit a sick friend; that her stepmother had gotten a note inviting her to do that. No one else could ever verify that. Lizzie made it up in order to keep people from finding her stepmother's corpse before she could turn dear old Daddy into the same insensate thing. That non-note was a giveaway. Lizzie was guilty. Those Andy prints were a giveaway. If he'd grabbed the butcher knife from the kitchen counter, as she claimed, Gloria's prints would have been on them, too.

But Roger and Gloria wanted to make sure. They wanted the world to know: Andrew and Andrew alone used that knife. They wiped it clean and put it in the hands of a corpse they'd already provided us with. Roger "needed" to shoot Andrew (of course he did if he *wanted* to have the merry widow all to himself). He was never especially logical, that Rog. Was Andrew really bent dead over that chair or did they place him there? Probably the former, but Andrew Drabble was framed and defamed and maimed. Andrew wasn't the only thing bent in Beloit. How did Gloria get him out to the house? Did she promise him some Lady Godivas and a big reconciliation? Or did she just give him the chance to play knight-errant by telling him that he, and he alone, could fix a faucet dripping dirty water as though it had been filtered through Frango Mints? Was she wearing her Shady Blonde disguise when he walked into the door, and if so what did he say? "My God, Gloria, you look as beautiful as ever even with that stupid wig on." Were these his last words ever? Well, few of us get to say anything profound right before we die. I read about one guy on Death Row who'd had ten years to prepare his final words, and when it came time all he could manage was something from the Bible. Andy wasn't original. Few of us are.

Of course they set me up, too, though my job wasn't to get killed but to witness the mysterious box bottom and so forth so that Andrew's faux identity as an obsessive husband could be established. Yeah, Roger was having his old partner on, but what is the old partner meant to do when the scam artist once saved his life?

I must admit that Roger's idea—it must have been his—to frame Andrew as a Drug Lord *was* pretty original, for Roger, I mean. He sensed that if the world kinda sorta thought that Andrew Drabble was Meth Royalty fewer people would care about what happened to him. And he was smart enough to make sure Shady Gloria always paid cash for the Robitussin and Energizer Bunnies. Oh, and remember that it was he, and he alone, who insisted that J&J really did have a Mr. Big to give us.

Oh, well, it was enough to fool everyone except for the Fat Guy Doomed to Go By Logic; the solitary chap who communes with a tabby. One late fall day I got up at about 4 and drove down to Aurora. Lieutenant Roger Webb had bought a nice place for himself on the city's north side, a little hacienda style place, a slightly imposing yellow brick mini-Alamo. It looked a bit more like a small mission than like a little house. I parked across the street and only had to wait for an hour for Gloria to walk out the flaming red front door and get into a purple Lexus—yeah, the same one, which was now Nyquil Bunny-free I'll wager—and drive off. She looked really happy. She didn't think she was hiding anything or needed to do so. Life was good. That robust Martha Stewart cheer was set on high. I doubt if she made any demands on Roger to be intimate. She thought he was a scheming hero, and he was. All those months he told Mary he was at the bar cogitating about his job he was with Gloria planning his happy fate.

I wonder if he ever told her about the time he saved my life.

I didn't wait for Roger. I didn't want to see him again. I had to get to work, and Beloit was 90 minutes north.

When I walked into the station Rose was waiting for me, pointed to her watch and told me I was tardy but that she'd not record it as such if, if I'd just listen to the latest.

"This morning she got out in this cold weather. She got out into the street. She had her big wrap on, but she made a big jam on Prairie Avenue. Cars were down to one lane because her chair had taken over the right lane. The uniforms had to block off traffic to remove her. They took her back to the apartment and told her never to do that again. She did it to get my goat. She knows I work here. She wants to ruin me. I'm going to kill her some day. No judge around here will condemn me."

She went on like that for another two or three minutes. No, I told her, I hadn't heard about this. I'd been in Aurora, Illinois, where the big casino was, getting evidence on a homicide that no one would listen to me about, and that I didn't want to do anything about anyhow. Of course I didn't tell Rose any of this. But I did speak, maybe, some kind of truth.

"You're at war, Rose. You're at war with Susan. She's at war with you. You know Phil and Gladys Wartenburg from over on Central? Yeah, them. The ones we have in here from time to time to cool them off from a domestic. Phil and Gladys; you and Susan: you're at war. But it gives your lives meaning, you see. War gives you a mission in life. Think of it that way, Rose. You've got a mission in life."

She put a roly-poly index finger on her third chin. This was the overweight woman as thinker. "And what about you, Jeremy? Are you at war? Do you have a mission?" She was pretty sarcastic. I don't think she liked my last speech. She'd wanted sympathy. I gave her philosophy, or was it just BS?

"I'm at war with nobody, Rose. And I have no mission." And I went to my cubicle. My new partner was not yet around.

That afternoon after work I did something bold. I decided to adopt a mission for myself, just like I'd adopted Dez once upon a time. I was thinking of sending Dez on a spy mission to Aurora, but I've got to admit that that's pretty far even for her. So I nixed the idea.

But back to that mission I was bound to adopt: By 5 it was dark. It was that time of year when the leaves are blowing around all the time and you think somebody's sneaking up on you. I always put a trembling hand on my piece when that happens. If I ever shoot a tree it'll be in November. It was warm, though, like a midnight in June or something.

I knocked on Roger's old door, not far from the local Episcopal church. Nothing. I had placed one plump foot in retreat when the door opened. It was Mary. Well, I expected it to be her.

Her face looked like it was on permanent strike. But the hairdo was still stunningly short, and she was still my girl if only she knew it and cared.

Then I knew who'd play her in the movie about this mess: Demi Moore.

"Jeremy? Hmmmm....come in, I suppose. I wasn't expecting you."

"You wouldn't be, no. Look, Mary, I won't stay long. I just wanted to see how you were and if there's anything I can do for you. The last few months have been rough, right?"

"You could say that, Jeremy. I lost my hero husband to the big city of Aurora. I'd lost him anyhow, even before he became a hero and long before Aurora. He stopped caring about me."

He'd ceased caring about me, too. The last thing Roger had ever said to me was in the halls of the station, between sessions of the interrogation among me and Charlie and him. He murmured to me: "I'm as clean as a tub full of Lysol, Jer."

"Anyhow," Mary went on, "I'm not good company so I hope you don't mind if I don't invite you for coffee or a drink."

I flinched. I didn't show it. I thought of Roger's last words to me about the Lysol and the tub.

"I don't think he stopped caring about you, Mary. I think of his last words he ever spoke to me."

"Yes?"

"Well, the very last word he spoke to me was your name. He said," I lied, "don't forget about Mary."

THE END

ABOUT THE AUTHOR

Tom McBride is co-author with Ron Nief of *The Mindset Lists of American History* (Wiley, 2011) and *The Mindset List of the Obscure* (Sourcebooks, 2014). He has authored as well four mystery novels (*Godawful Dreams, Rox & Darlene, The Homicide At Malahide* and *The Curious Old Men of Belial College*). *Godawful Dreams* was featured on public radio's Chapter A Day during summer of 2016. He is also author of *The Great American Lay: An All Too Brief History of Sex,* and *When You Could Only Dribble Once: 51 Famously Forgotten Game-Changers*, which features among others Beloit College's great coach Bill Knapton.

Made in the USA
Lexington, KY
06 December 2017